16c

"Catherine Palmer's writing shines with romance
and the inner struggles of the heart."
—Francine Rivers, bestselling author of
Redeeming Love

"Catherine Palmer...understands hurts as well as joys,
and portrays them authentically and insightfully."
—Randy Alcorn, bestselling author of *Deadline*

"*Love's Haven* is a glorious story that was
wonderfully told by Catherine Palmer.... I couldn't
devour this story fast enough. The characters
immediately took up residence in my heart,
and I felt every emotion they felt. Catherine Palmer
did a stand-up job of describing each scene and
creating a world which no reader will want to leave.
This bestselling author will definitely have a place
on my favorites list."
—*Cataromance Reviews*

PRAISE FOR GAIL GAYMER MARTIN

"*The Christmas Kite* is a tender romance,
the story of two wounded people learning to live and
love again. And I guarantee that little Mac will steal your
heart. Settle into your favorite chair and enjoy."
—Robin Lee Hatcher, bestselling author of
Loving Libby

"In *The Christmas Kite*, Gail Martin probes
the depths of love and forgiveness.
A tender and heartwarming read."
—Lyn Cote, bestselling author of *Chloe*

"Gail Gaymer Martin's best book to date.
Real conflict and very likeable characters
enhance this wonderful romantic story."
—*Romantic Times* on *Loving Hearts*

CATHERINE PALMER

is a bestselling author and winner of the Christy Award for her outstanding Christian romance. She also received the Career Achievement Award for Inspirational Fiction from *Romantic Times*. Raised in Kenya, she lives in Missouri with her husband and their two sons.

GAIL GAYMER MARTIN

is an award-winning author for Steeple Hill and Barbour Publishing. She is the recipient of a *Romantic Times* Reviewer's Choice Award, and her novel *The Christmas Kite* has been optioned for television by Hallmark. Visit Gail at www.gailmartin.com or write to her at P.O. Box 760063, Lathrup Village, MI 48076.

CATHERINE PALMER

GAIL GAYMER MARTIN

THAT CHRISTMAS FEELING

Steeple
Hill®

Published by Steeple Hill Books™

STEEPLE HILL BOOKS

Steeple
Hill®

ISBN 0-373-78545-3

THAT CHRISTMAS FEELING

Copyright © 2005 by Harlequin Books S.A.

The publisher acknowledges the copyright holders
of the individual works as follows:

CHRISTMAS IN MY HEART
Copyright © 2004 by Catherine Palmer

CHRISTMAS MOON
Copyright © 2004 by Gail Gaymer Martin

Printed in U.S.A.

CONTENTS

CHRISTMAS IN MY HEART   9
Catherine Palmer

CHRISTMAS MOON   141
Gail Gaymer Martin

CHRISTMAS IN MY HEART

Catherine Palmer

"I will honor Christmas in my heart
and try to keep it all the year."
—Ebenezer Scrooge in *A Christmas Carol*
by Charles Dickens

For the other three FABs:
BB Heil, Lucia Kincheloe and Kristie McGonegal.
Thanks for supporting me, praying with me
and loving me these many years.

I love you all!

Chapter One

Never again, Claire Ross fumed as she stepped through the front door onto the porch of her aunt Flossie's house. So much for spreading the Christmas spirit. Lifting the fragrant pine wreath she had brought as a gift, Claire jammed it onto a nail in the door and stomped across the sagging wooden floorboards.

She had never met a more irascible, heartless, crusty old windbag! The woman was impossible. Picking her way down the damp and splintered steps, Claire vowed that this first time she had visited her great-aunt would also be the last. No wonder the entire Ross family had disowned Florence Ross. She deserved it.

"And stay gone!" a voice crowed behind her.

Claire swung around in time to see Aunt Flossie point a double-barreled shotgun into the gray Missouri sky and pull the trigger. At the deafening blast, a pair of doves fluttered screeching out of a nearby oak tree, five yowling cats hightailed it from under the porch and every dog in a three-mile radius of Buffalo, Missouri, began to bark. Stunned, Claire watched as her aunt grabbed the Christmas wreath off the front door and sent it sailing like a Frisbee across the yard.

"Don't need Christmas 'round here!" Aunt Flossie shouted. "Don't need it, don't want it!"

Breathing hard, Claire stared at the tiny, white-haired woman. Flossie wore a faded pink bathrobe with its terry-cloth loops picked into long strings by the horde of cats that lived in and around old Ross Mansion. The robe's hem hung uneven and frayed around her thin ivory calves. Socks—one navy, the other black—were rolled to her ankles. And a pair of men's leather work boots with steel toes and untied laces anchored her feet.

Hair splayed out like dandelion fluff, Flossie stared at her niece. Her sharp blue eyes narrowed as her mouth turned down. "This is my property," she sneered. "You stay off!"

"Believe me, I have no intention of ever—"

A wailing siren drowned out Claire's words as a blue car sped toward them down the narrow paved road. Emblazoned with the word *Police* in bold white letters on the side, the squad car pulled to a stop beside the gray picket fence that surrounded Flossie Ross's yard. The siren died, the driver's door swung open and a man Claire instantly recognized as Robert West, Buffalo's police chief, stepped out.

"Miss Ross," he called as he rounded the fence and strode down the driveway. "How many times have I told you not to go firing guns inside city limits? Now, give me that thing!"

"You can't have it, you ol' turkey buzzard!" Shaking the weapon, Flossie tottered down the steps. "Get outta my yard!"

Claire's fury at her aunt shifted to concern as the chief stalked toward the old woman. Rob West was not a man to defy. Six feet four inches tall, broad shouldered and narrow hipped, he had been quarterback of Buffalo High School's winning football team and a state-champion wrestler. Though Claire had returned to her hometown the previous summer and had been teaching high school history since the start of the fall semester, she had yet to cross paths with Rob.

Not that she'd been looking for him. In school, Rob had been a popular, handsome athlete and the beloved boyfriend of the prettiest, blondest, curviest girl in their class—the sweetheart he had married the day after his graduation from the police academy. Until a teacher paired the two mismatched freshmen for an ongoing four-year research project, Rob had paid scant attention to Claire Ross with her coarse red hair, ghostly pale skin and rail-thin body. It didn't help that she adored school, loved to read and made it perfectly clear she thought Rob West was as dumb as a Missouri mule.

Still, they had somehow ended up becoming friends—easily teasing each other, sharing ideas and even confiding secrets. He called her Clarence and sneaked her pieces of her favorite brand of bubble gum. She called him a nincompoop and a lamebrain, and she blew bubbles, which he mashed onto her nose.

In the course of the four years, Claire made sure the research project progressed, and eventually she even convinced Rob that Buffalo's role in the Civil War really was an interesting topic. He made sure the other guys didn't malign skinny Claire behind her back, and she actually ended up getting a date to her senior prom.

"What are you shooting at today, Miss Ross?" Rob asked. "Is a stray dog after your cats? Or are you mad at the garbage truck again?"

"It's her." Flossie pointed a thin finger at Claire. "She's trespassing on my property."

Rob's bright blue eyes focused for the first time on the younger woman. His brow furrowed as he took off his hat. "Claire Ross? Is that you?"

"Of course it's me," she said. "I drove all the way over here to bring my aunt a Christmas gift, and she—"

"She started right off griping about my cats!" Flossie cut in.

"Everybody in town gripes about your cats," Rob retorted. "You're in violation of city ordinances, Miss Ross. Only four cats are allowed per household. A city license is required. You've got to have proof of current rabies vaccinations for each cat. And it's against municipal code to allow your pets to run loose off your property."

"So what? They're not my cats anyhow. People drop 'em here, and I take 'em in." She gave a loud snort and shouted, "I'm a kindhearted animal lover, that's all!"

"How many cats do you have now? It was sixteen the last time I came out here."

"Who cares? Sixteen or twenty, what difference does it make? They're not doing harm to anyone."

"They stink, Miss Ross. Plain and simple, you've got an odor problem. Not only that, but your property is a public eyesore. You've got cats on the roof, cats in the trees, cats in the basement—"

"Not in the basement. I keep that locked."

"The point is, ma'am, you've got to get rid of some of the cats and clean up this place."

"Or what? You ain't out here about the cats anyhow. You're here to get that woman off my land!"

Rob glanced at Claire again. His face registered surprise for a second time, as if he'd failed to remember her from a moment before. She clamped her hands on her hips in frustration. Bad enough that she had been invisible in high school. But now? At twenty-eight, she thought she had improved a tad. She filled out her clothes in the right places, she had earned a master's degree in history, she had been the assistant curator at a museum in Savannah, Georgia, and despite recently having her wedding canceled only a month before it was scheduled, she certainly had plenty of confidence.

"I'd heard you were back in town," Rob said. "Teaching history at the high school, someone told me."

"And trying to be a kind niece." She glanced down at the pine wreath. It lay half in a puddle of icy water and half in the mud. Bright red berries, pretty ribbons and silver bells were forlornly buried in the fragrant branches. "It's real, you know. I bought it at the florist shop and brought it over here for my aunt. I hoped it would cheer her up."

"Cheer Miss Ross? You've got your work cut out for you there." His mouth tilted into a grin. "But as I recall, Clarence, you never objected to hard work."

So he did remember her after all. To her dismay, Claire felt her cheeks grow warm. "Well, I just didn't expect—"

"You planning to arrest that woman, Chief West?" Flossie demanded. "She's the one in violation of city code. She's trespassing!"

Rob turned to the older woman again. "Miss Ross, Claire is your niece. It's almost Christmas, and she's trying to be neighborly."

"Neighborly? I didn't ask her to come over. I never invited her—and I don't want her!" Flossie shook her fist. "Now, you just make her get off my land, because I don't tolerate…"

"Did you actually go inside the house?" Rob asked Claire as her aunt ranted and stomped around on the porch. "I've never been able to get through the front door."

Claire nodded. "The smell is awful. It can't be sanitary."

"I've sent social workers over here to check on her, but she won't let them inside."

"I barely set foot in the foyer before she went after her gun. All I saw was torn wallpaper, piles of newspapers and cats. Lots of cats."

Claire mused for a moment, recalling stories she had heard told around the family dinner table. A clapboard confection of nineteenth-century turrets, gables, balconies and gingerbread, the old house had been built by a wealthy Ross ancestor in anticipation of a promised railroad that never came to town. Generations came and went, and the family fortune dwindled. Now only Florence Ross and her cats remained in the dilapidated, sagging structure.

"When I was a girl," Claire told Rob, "my father used to say that Ross Mansion was a showpiece inside. He believed it was filled with family treasures—artwork, antiques, historical items. But if that's true, everything is probably ruined."

"I'm afraid so." Rob's blue eyes clouded. "Your aunt is an animal hoarder, Claire. It's part of the spectrum of mental illnesses known as obsessive-compulsive disorders. Miss Ross collects cats. Most of them are feral. She can't turn them away, she won't get them neutered or spayed and they've infested the house and grounds. People call me at all hours of the night to complain. The cats yowl and fight and dig up gardens and tear into trash cans—"

A second shotgun blast shattered the conversation and set the dogs barking all over again. "Hey, both of you trespassers!" Flossie screeched. "Get out!"

"That does it." Rob swung around and marched up onto the porch. "Hand over your weapon. Do it now, Miss Ross, or I'll take you in."

With one hand he grabbed the shotgun. With the other he dipped into the gaping pocket of Flossie's shaggy pink robe and took out a fistful of unspent shells.

"I've got a rifle inside the house!" she squalled at him. "It's a .22, and I've got a pistol, too. I have the right to bear arms!"

"Not in my town you don't. Not anymore." He stepped around her and pushed open the front door. "I'll just go in there and—"

"Don't go in! Don't go in!"

He vanished, the old woman scurrying through the door behind him. Claire let out a breath. But her relief evaporated when Rob reappeared again immediately, his face contorted.

"That house is a public menace," he scolded Flossie, who stood glaring up at him. "I can't even breathe in there without a face mask."

"Good!" she snapped back. "Don't breathe. You can just die, for all I care!"

"Miss Ross, your neighbors have been pestering me about you for years, but I've been patient. Too patient. Today you've pushed me over the edge. I want this place cleaned up by Christmas, or I'll ask the city to condemn it and evict you. The cats have to go. The waste has to be cleaned up—and I don't mean with mop water. You'd better get some disinfectant. And paint. I want you to paint these outside walls and the picket fence, too. You hear me?"

"I don't hear a thing!"

"And no more gunshots!"

As he strode toward his squad car, Claire caught his arm. "Wait, Rob, you can't do this! Aunt Flossie is too old to clean and paint the house. And she's too mean to obey you."

"Then we'll have to evict her."

"How can you even say that? If you turn her out of the house, what's to become of her?"

"She can move in with you," he retorted.

"Are you crazy?" she called after him as he opened his car door.

"Not as crazy as your aunt."

As the blue car made a U-turn and sped off in a cloud of dust, Claire clenched her jaw. That dumb Rob West always had been too big for his britches! What an ego—calling Buffalo *his* town, threatening to evict Aunt Flossie and ordering Claire to take her in. As if Claire would ever consider opening her pristine little bungalow, her precious sanctuary and refuge, to that impossible woman and her umpteen smelly cats!

No way. Absolutely not! She owed Aunt Flossie nothing. The woman had never played any part in Claire's life. A lifelong spinster, Flossie had avoided family gatherings, never invited anyone over and certainly made it clear she wanted to be left alone. So clear, in fact, that the whole Ross family had readily agreed to deed her their stakes in the mansion. Despite its rumored treasures, the house held no claim on anyone's affections. Not if that meant encountering Florence Ross and her bitter, biting tongue.

"He stole my gun!" Flossie fumed, turning her small blue eyes on her great-niece. "Did you see that? The police chief stole my shotgun!"

Claire hesitated. Her urge to rebuke the bedraggled creature was mitigated only by the knowledge that Rob West always meant exactly what he said. If Flossie didn't get rid of the cats and clean up the house, he would have it condemned. Claire's parents were out of town for the winter, and as her great-aunt's nearest living relative, she would then become legally responsible for the elderly woman.

"Aunt Flossie, do you know who I am?" she asked.

"Of course I do. You're Jim's girl. Listen, you better tell your daddy to get his sorry hide over to the police station and bring me back my shotgun!"

Picking up the muddy wreath, Claire shook her head in frustration. She had come here to be kind, not to take abuse. Life had been difficult enough lately. While preparing for her wedding only nine months before, Claire had learned that her fiancé was seeing another woman. After canceling the nuptials, she'd stayed on in her job at the museum as long as she could. But her deep-seated unhappiness had convinced her she needed a new beginning.

At first the idea of coming home to Missouri felt like a step backward. When her mother mentioned that a teaching position had opened up in Buffalo, Claire immediately rejected the idea. She was a museum curator, not a high school history teacher. And she had no interest in returning to the little town she once had so eagerly fled. But the chance to escape the pain of her broken engagement and start life over changed her mind. After talking with her pastor and praying about the situation, she had embraced the opportunity and made the move.

As it turned out, Claire found she enjoyed teaching and appreciated Buffalo far more than she'd expected. Most important, as the darkness in her heart began to fade, a new dream took its place. Why not open a small museum dedicated to the town's unique history? To that end, Claire already had approached several of the city aldermen. If they could find a suitable location, she explained, then she would help gather the necessary historical artifacts and set up displays. Volunteers could staff the museum during visiting hours. Local schoolchildren certainly would benefit, and a small entrance fee might help the museum pay for its upkeep. Though the aldermen were skeptical that such an expense could be justified, they had agreed to look into it.

Feeling a bit lonely as the holidays approached, Claire had been trying to make herself reach out into the community. She joined her church's special Christmas choir, attended a play, even accepted a position on a committee. Bringing the wreath as a gift for her great-aunt had seemed a perfect way to honor the holiness of the season and to express her own newfound hope that her life had truly taken a turn for the better.

Now this.

Claire took a step toward the porch. "My father isn't in town, Aunt Flossie. The day after Thanksgiving my parents drove their RV to Texas to spend the winter. No one else is here, either. Dad's brother, Jake, moved to St. Louis three years ago. And his sister, Johanna, is on a mission trip to Haiti until next summer. I'm the only Ross around. So it's just you and me."

Flossie bent over and picked up a gray-and-white-striped cat. "Well, go on home, then," she said, her voice softening as she rubbed her cheek against the animal's fur. "I don't need you or any of the rest of 'em."

"You're planning to paint the house by yourself?" Claire stepped onto the porch. The odor emanating from the open front door would have made a skunk swoon. "And clean it up? And get rid of all the cats? That's what Chief West said you have to do."

"I don't care what that ol' buzzard said." Flossie set the cat back on its feet. "This is my house."

"Yes, but he has the power to condemn it. And he's only given you two weeks."

"Who cares? I have the deed to this house! It's mine!" She frowned as Claire stepped past her and went into the foyer again. "Hey, what are you doing? Get out! Get out of my house!"

"Oh, no…oh, Aunt Flossie…" Claire gritted her teeth to keep from gagging as she edged around a waist-high stack of newspapers. Swags of cobwebs draped from the chandelier overhead. Was it crystal? Impossible to tell with all the dust. The wallpaper, once a flocked velvet maroon in an Oriental pattern, hung in shreds. Fraying ropes held cockeyed pictures in heavy gilt frames, their art obscured by soot and dirt. The rug had rotted out from under the piles of damp newspapers, and everywhere lay evidence that the cats had ceased to use their litter boxes years ago.

"Aunt Flossie, this is…" Claire tried to think of adequate words. "Well, it's just—"

"Just *get out* is what it is! I didn't invite you in! I don't want you, and I don't need you!"

"And I don't care!" Rounding on the much smaller woman, Claire jabbed a finger at her. "You're stuck with me, Aunt Flossie. You can either clean up this disgusting mess, or that nincompoop Rob West will turn you out of the house and make me take care of you! Do you understand that? Do you see that you have no choice in this, and neither do I?"

Flossie's narrow lips went white. "I heard the man. I'm not deaf."

"Then what do you plan to do about it?"

"Why, I'll clean it, of course."

"You will?" Her aunt's capitulation stunned Claire. "You'll throw out all the newspapers? And you'll wash the floors?"

"With disinfectant."

Claire eyed her. "What about the cats?"

"Fare-thee-well to the cats." Flossie flipped her hand in a jaunty wave. "I'll call the animal shelter to come get 'em."

"All of them?"

"Every one."

Letting out a breath, Claire set the wreath on an old chair with upholstery that had been clawed to shreds. "Fine, then. I won't bother you anymore."

"Good."

Grateful, she stepped back out onto the porch. "Because it's really not healthy for you in there, Aunt Flossie," she said, feeling a little guilty about the relief she felt. "It's not safe for your food, for one thing. I mean...do you have enough to eat? Do you need anything, because I could—"

The door slammed shut in her face. Claire stared at it for a moment, fighting fury, biting back rage.

"And a merry Christmas to you, too!" she called out as she turned and headed for her car.

Rob West took his seat at the far end of the long polished oak table, directly across from Mayor Clement

Bloom. The last place he wanted to be on a frosty December night was tucked away in the dank county courthouse basement with the mayor and a bunch of other community-spirited citizens. Not that planning the Christmas parade didn't rank fairly high on his priority list.

Rob enjoyed his role as a public servant, because it meant getting out of the office and mingling with Buffalo's residents. Every able-bodied man, woman and child in the area always turned out for the annual parade—police sirens wailing, fire trucks blasting their horns, floats rolling by, endless thrown candy soaring through the air. Not only did the police force cordon off streets and control traffic, but the chief of police traditionally joined the mayor in leading the procession through town. The Christmas parade created the perfect opportunity to promote goodwill, and Rob welcomed it.

But tonight his focus was elsewhere. Trouble had come to Buffalo. Throughout the fall the local police, the highway patrol and the Dallas County Sheriff's Department had noted an increase in methamphetamine traffic in the region. Somebody was cooking and distributing the illegal drug. But who? And where?

Methamphetamine manufacturing had become one of Missouri law enforcement's biggest headaches. The largely rural state provided meth makers with an ideal setup. From farmers' fertilizer tanks they stole a primary raw ingredient for the drug. And they used the many isolated farms and forests as hideouts in which to cook the highly explosive and pungent mix. As the public's appetite for the drug grew, meth manufacturing had gradually crawled into Missouri's towns and cities. But until this year, Rob had seen very little activity in his territory, and he was grateful.

His force—an assistant chief, a corporal, five patrolmen and a secretary—had more than enough to handle as it was. Domestic altercations were the most common of their calls. Petty stealing cropped up now and then. And traffic accidents sometimes occurred around five in the evening when cars attempted to negotiate the narrow streets of the town that formed the junction of U.S. Highway 65 and Missouri Highway 32.

"Well, I guess this committee probably ought to come to order," Mayor Bloom spoke up. A hefty fellow with a big mustache, Clement Bloom was Buffalo's lone veterinarian. "Who's here? Let's see, we've got Chief West, a'course. Mrs. Hopper, you represent the board of Realtors, right? Jerry, you're speaking for the downtown merchants. By the way, the store windows look real good this year."

"I think so, too, Mayor." The owner of the local drugstore grinned. "The middle school art classes came to the square and painted them."

Rob checked his watch. He had two men out patrolling side streets and alleyways in search of any suspicious activity. As soon as the parade meeting ended, he would join them in his own squad car. The past few weeks, he had worked far into the night in the hope of ferreting out the source of the methamphetamine that was entering his jurisdiction. But so far, few clues had crossed his radar screen.

"We've got silver bells and green holly and gold stars,"

Jerry was saying. "It's not just your usual Santas and rein-
deer. There's even a window with a scene from Dickens's
A Christmas Carol. You know, Tiny Tim and Scrooge and
everyone. I thought the kids were real creative with their
painting this year."

"Any complaints about the manger scene on the barbershop window, Mayor?" One of the local pastors had come
to the meeting to represent the ministerial alliance. Vari-
ous church choirs would be performing on the parade
floats. "Last year someone griped that the schoolchildren
shouldn't be allowed to paint Bible scenes—due to the separation of church and state."

"And we all know who made *that* complaint," Mrs.
Hopper put in.

Rob nodded along with the others around the table. Jack
Granger, the local atheist, liked to voice his opinions in the
newspaper and at city council meetings. Every town had
its colorful characters, Rob realized. Buffalo enjoyed perhaps more than its fair share. In addition to Granger, they
had "The Walker," a fellow who claimed he had been
wounded in Vietnam and had a steel plate in his head.
They had Mr. Chin, an Asian gentleman who appeared out
of nowhere every now and then. Wearing white gloves and
a black hat, Mr. Chin strolled around the square, peered
into shop windows, got himself a haircut at the barbershop
and vanished again. And then there was Florence Ross.

The image of the vituperative old woman had barely entered Rob's head when the meeting room's door swung
open and Flossie's niece stepped in.

"Sorry I'm late," Claire Ross said, pulling off a pair of bright blue wool gloves. "The high school secretary gave me a message that we were meeting at the public library, so I went over there. When nobody showed up, I made a few phone calls and found out you were here. Whew!"

She let out a breath and smiled broadly—until her eyes fell on Rob. Instantly serious, she pulled off her hat, releasing a billow of auburn curls, and took the only chair available. Right next to his.

"Good evening, Chief West," she said in a low voice, flashing her green eyes at him. "No one told me you were on this committee."

"I'm on all the committees. It's part of the job."

Hard as he tried not to, Rob couldn't help staring at the woman beside him. What had become of skinny Claire Ross with her too-big mouth, her pasty white face and her straight hair that stuck out in all kinds of strange directions? And who had replaced her with this curvaceous, full-lipped, porcelain-skinned, redheaded beauty?

Ol' Clarence had never sported curls in high school. And those eyes! Hadn't they once been a sort of muddy olive? Tonight they sparkled like emeralds as she glanced across the table.

"What?" she whispered, flipping the word at him. "Have you forgotten who I am again?"

"You didn't used to have curls."

"That's because I ironed my hair." She shrugged. "I gave that up in college. Quit staring, you lamebrain. It's me."

He tore his focus from her and tried to concentrate on

the mayor, who was outlining the parade route. Bloom was famous for his visual aids, and tonight he had brought along a map drawn in black marker on a large sheet of neon-green poster board. He held a laser pen to create a tiny white directional point.

"Now, we'll have the marching bands gather over here in the usual spot," he was saying. "And the floats—"

"Excuse me, Mayor, but you've put the bank on the wrong corner of the square." All eyes turned to the speaker, Mrs. Hopper. "In my work as a real estate agent I see a lot of maps, and this one is incorrect, sir. The bank should be across the street."

The mayor studied his carefully executed drawing. "Well, I'll be. Are you sure?"

Rob leaned toward Claire. "What do you mean, you ironed your hair?"

"With an iron. On an ironing board." She tipped her head to one side and demonstrated. "Straight hair was in style."

He eyed the curls that bounced and bobbled down her shoulders and onto her soft blue sweater. Clarence Ross had curls. How about that?

"So, what do you think, Chief West? Uh…*Rob?*" The mayor leaned over and cleared his throat. "About blocking off the streets around the school? Will that be a problem?"

Collecting himself, Rob stared at the map and tried to make sense of it. "We'll block off the usual streets. Just like every year."

"But we were discussing the idea of moving the marching bands over here." He pointed at the green poster board. "Because what I was saying was that the local cable company has asked to have a float this year. And several clubs at the high school want to do floats, too. Isn't that right, Miss Ross?"

Claire pulled a sheet of paper from her purse. "That's correct, Mayor Bloom. The Spanish club and the chess club each would like to create a float."

"The chess club?" Mrs. Hopper frowned. "What kind of a float can that be? Kids playing chess? What's interesting about that?"

"The students are planning to make large chess-piece costumes and walk around on the float as though it's a chessboard. It's a way to draw attention to their club, which they feel doesn't get as much community support as athletics."

"No question about *that*," Mayor Bloom said.

Bloom had never played on a school sports team, and Rob had considered him the quintessential nerd. That is, until he'd returned to town with "D.V.M." attached to his name and set up a bustling veterinary clinic. Nothing nerdy about that.

"All right, Miss Ross, we'll let the two clubs build floats," Bloom continued, "if you'll speak to the school superintendent about our parking problems."

"Certainly," she said. "I'm sure we can work something out. And I would think the police force can figure out how to adapt to the changes, even though it might be a little confusing for them at first."

Rob stiffened at the dig. "No problem, Mayor."

"Well, I guess we're about done here, then. Mrs. Hopper has typed up the order of entries in the parade. Like always, she put a float or two between each of the marching bands. She's got the squad car with the chief and me leading the parade, and the fire truck with Santa at the end. Looks like it's all in good shape. You can go ahead and hand out copies of your list, Mrs. Hopper. The police are on board to control the traffic, and Miss Ross will take care of the parking issue. We've got city sanitation set up to clean the streets after the horses. There's always a lot of candy wrappers lying around, too. And finally, we've got the parade route worked out." He eyed his neon map again for a moment. "I'll move the bank to the correct corner for the diagram that'll go in the newspaper. Anything else? All right, then we're adjourned. See you at the parade."

Chairs scraped back across the tile floor as Mrs. Hopper passed around her list of parade entries. Never much good at sitting for long periods, Rob stood and stretched his muscles. Claire was speaking to the preacher as she pulled on her gloves and hat. Rob considered walking away without another word to her, but the woman had clearly baited him with that crack about his police force. Besides, he had a little matter to lob back at her.

"Excuse me, Miss Ross," he said as she made to sashay past him without even a flick of her green eyes. "Do you have a minute?"

She paused, and the pink in her cheeks brightened as she faced him. "If this is about my hair—"

"It's about your aunt, Florence Ross. The cats are still

on her property, I'm still getting phone calls in the night and when the wind is right, you can smell her house clear across town. I gave her till Christmas to clean up the place. Time is slipping away fast. But you're smart enough to know all that already, so I just wanted to make sure you'll be available to take her with you when I go over to condemn the place."

The blush drained away as fast as it had come. "Aunt Flossie hasn't done anything?"

"Nope. As I told you before, she has a mental illness. The cats are the focus of her obsessive-compulsive disorder. There's no way she'll give them up without a fight."

"But she told me…" She pursed her lips. The room had cleared out now, and she raised her voice. "Rob West, I always knew you were thick, but I never thought you were mean!"

"For your information, I am not thick." Setting his fists at his waist, he took a step toward her. "And you know good and well I'm not mean. It's my job to uphold the law—"

"By throwing a helpless old lady out onto the streets in the middle of winter?"

"Flossie's not helpless. She has you."

"She doesn't want me. And I don't want her, either."

"Now who's mean?" He shook his head. "Have you forgotten what you used to tell me, Claire? You grew up in that fairy-tale family who went to church every time the doors opened. And you used to preach at me, remember?"

"I did not preach."

"You preached all the time. You'd say, 'Rob West,

you've got to do your homework if you ever want to amount to anything…. You'd better stop that cussing, because civilized people don't swear…. I won't have you taking the Lord's name in vain in front of me, Rob West…. If you want to turn into a decent human being, Rob, you ought to go to church and quit messing around with Sherry and drinking with your buddies after the game.'"

As he spoke, Claire's mouth slowly fell open. She folded her hands together, and the hard emerald in her eyes softened to mossy green. "I don't remember any of that," she told him.

"Well, I do. I remember every bit of it. And most of all, I remember that you told me I had to take care of people. You said loving people was a lot more important than winning state football championships and wrestling trophies. Caring about the needy, the hungry, the homeless was what God expected of us, and it was all that really mattered in the long run."

When she didn't speak, he continued. "I thought you were the goofiest, dorkiest girl I'd ever known. But I listened to you, Claire, because everything you ever said to me made sense. Your words took me all the way to the police academy, where I was trained to do exactly what you said—take care of people. Because of your preaching at me, I married Sherry when I got her pregnant and she threatened to have an abortion. I stayed with her even though we lost our baby and the marriage was rocky all the way to the day she died in a car accident two years ago. The words you said to me over and over for four long years of working on that never-ending research project took me to church and led me to give up trying to control my life and to surrender it to Jesus Christ."

She moistened her lips, her eyes fastened to him. "Rob, I—"

"And now you're telling me you don't want to take care of your aunt? You won't look after an elderly mentally ill woman with no family but you? What happened to you, Claire? Where's the girl I knew in high school?"

She pushed her purse strap up onto her shoulder. "This isn't high school, Rob. People do change. And besides, you have no idea what I've been through. You don't know anything about me."

"Yes, I do. I know you're still smart, you're about a hundred times prettier and you're mean."

"I am not mean!"

"Excuse me, but I have to turn out the lights and lock up." He stepped around her.

"I am not mean!" she repeated, following him to the door and up the stairs to the main level. "I've worked very hard to recover from my own issues, I'll have you know."

"Issues." He flipped off a main switch, instantly casting them into darkness.

"Yes, issues. My fiancé left me for another woman, I had to quit the job I'd trained for and loved, and now I'm back in this little podunk town trying to start over. I have a tiny house, but it's mine. It's my home, and I'm not letting some ornery old woman who never cared about me or any of my family move in!"

They stepped out of the courthouse into the night. "Like I said, Clarence. You're mean."

As he walked away, she called after him. "My name is Claire!"

"Rence," he shouted back.

"Claire!"

"Rence!" He got into his squad car and backed out into the street. How about that, he thought as he drove off to look for meth dealers. Claire Ross had had those curls all along.

Chapter Two

Just as Claire pulled her car to a stop in front of Ross Mansion, a cascade of light, fluffy snowflakes began. Like goose down from a torn pillow, the white clumps gathered on the windshield and danced across the car's hood. She paused, soaking in the heater's comforting warmth before finally switching off the engine. For a moment she dropped her forehead onto her gloved hands that still clutched the steering wheel.

"Not what I want to do," she murmured through clenched teeth. "Are you hearing me, God? This is *not* what I want to do today! I don't like Aunt Flossie. I don't want to help her. And I'm furious with Rob West for shaming me into this! But I'm here, Lord, bad attitude and all. You promised to work things out for the good of people who love You and are called according to Your purpose. I do love You, and I know You want me to be kind to my great-aunt. So, please…even though I realize I'm doing this badly…please help me."

Letting out a long sigh, Claire opened the car door and stepped into the snowy morning. Bitter Missouri wind instantly penetrated her heavy winter jacket to the very marrow of her bones. Her cheeks ached. Her fingers went numb. Her eyes watered. Even her teeth hurt.

Shivering, she trotted across the yard, her boots crunching on the frozen crabgrass that no doubt would bloom with a sea of golden dandelions in the spring. Good grief, what was wrong with Florence Ross that she couldn't at least have a decent yard?

After living near the ocean with its difficult climate and soil, Claire had come to appreciate that in Missouri, people tended their perfect postage-stamp lots with the loving care a mother gave a newborn child. They fertilized, weeded and reseeded until thick green grass covered every inch of ground. They sodded, dethatched and aerated. They planted flowers and bushes and trees, and they spread decorative mulch around everything that rose more than an inch above the smooth plane of their lawns. If all that wasn't enough to satisfy, Missourians liked to add trellises, fountains, birdbaths, gazebos and collections of concrete statues—gnomes and cherubs and fairies. Early in the morning elderly ladies could be spotted with their dandelion forks, rooting out the pestilent weed with the passion of zealots. And nothing made a Missouri man prouder than to circle his yard several times a week atop his riding lawn mower.

Florence Ross, on the other hand, seemed determined to cultivate the perfect breeding ground for every dandelion seed, crabgrass root and burr that made its way into her neighbors' yards. Claire knocked on her aunt's door a second time. No doubt those three cats huddled up against the outside of the brick chimney joined their feline companions in spreading fleas, chiggers and ticks everywhere they roamed. Not to mention dragging scraps of garbage from the trash cans into one yard or another.

"Aunt Flossie!" she shouted. "Open up! I'm freezing out here."

No wonder the townspeople reviled the elderly spinster. Claire felt sure that everyone up and down this street would be thrilled if the police chief condemned Ross Mansion and kicked Flossie out. But the very thought of the foul-tempered woman ever setting foot inside Claire's clean, quiet house sent prickles of horror down her spine. It also had motivated her to hurry over this Saturday morning and start rounding up Aunt Flossie's feral felines.

"Hey!" she hollered, hammering with her fist on the solid oak door. "Aunt Flossie, you'd better come down here and—"

"Get offa my property!" The door opened an inch, and the barrel of a .22 rifle slid through the gap. "And I mean business!"

Claire stepped back and swallowed a gulp of surprise. Okay, this was another gun. Yes, indeed. And most certainly it would be loaded.

"Aunt Flossie?" she croaked out. "Uh, it's me. Your niece, Claire Ross."

"I know who y'are. I told you not to come back here!"

"But you also told me—"

"Then get off my porch!" The door opened wider, and Flossie glared as she brandished the rifle. "I don't want you here!"

"And I don't want to be here," Claire snapped back. She grabbed the rifle barrel as she had seen Rob do, and stepped to one side. "You promised to get rid of the cats and clean up this place, Aunt Flossie. You promised!"

"I don't give a bucket of spit what I said! Let go of my gun and—"

"You let go! I'm here to round up cats. I've brought a net and a pet carrier, and every last one of them—"

The gun went off with a deafening boom, jerking out of Claire's hand and blowing a hole through the porch roof. Claire jumped backward as though she herself had been shot. Flossie wobbled for a moment, then toppled to her knees. The .22 clattered onto the icy porch.

"Get out!" Flossie screeched, her fingers gripping the filthy marble threshold. "Get off my land!"

"You nearly hit me, you crazy coot!" Claire smacked open the door with her hand. "You could have killed me! Now, get up off that floor, Aunt Flossie. And don't even think about going for the rifle."

As the woman reached out for the gun, Claire kicked it across the porch. It spun on the slick wood, sliding in circles until it dropped off the steps and into the yard. Vaguely aware of an approaching siren, Claire stepped over her aunt and into the reeking foyer of the aging mansion.

"Get up, Aunt Flossie!" she commanded. "You're not

going to shoot me. I am going to round up your cats—and you're going to help me."

Her aunt was still on the floor, crouching on hands and knees. "Get away from me," she huffed. "Go on. Get outta here."

"Aunt Flossie, you have no choice in this." Claire glanced out across the yard at the squad car pulling to a stop. "Now you've brought the police again. Oh, great, it's Rob West. Well, this is just perfect. He'll probably throw you out right this minute, and I'll have to… Aunt Flossie?"

Needles of alarm shot through Claire as she knelt beside the woman still huddled in the doorway. Unmoving, Flossie breathed heavily, her wispy hair drifting in the chill wind that sucked around the corner of the old house. Claire laid her hand on her aunt's back. A knobby ridge defined her spine, and her shoulder blades stood out beneath the ragged pink bathrobe.

"Aunt Flossie, are you all right?" Claire asked softly.

A gnarled hand shot out and clapped her on the shoulder. "Back off before I have to coldcock ya! Look what you did—busted both my knees. Elbones, too, probably."

"I never touched you. You fell when you shot off that—" Claire bit off her retort. "Oh, never mind. Just let me help you up before we both freeze."

As she reached around her aunt's scarecrow frame, a pair of boots thudded toward them across the porch floor. "Good morning, ladies," Rob said. "Would one of you care to explain—"

"She fell," Claire cut in. "What does it look like?"

"She pushed me," Flossie spat out, her breath fogging the marble threshold. "Knocked me down and broke both my knees!"

"I did *not*—"

"Just be quiet, both of you." Muttering in disgust, Rob scooped Flossie into his arms and headed through the front door. "The apple doesn't fall far from the tree is all I can say."

"What is that supposed to mean?" Claire demanded, following him into the foyer and slamming the door shut behind them. Rob made for a room from which came the only evidence of warmth in the mansion. "Because I'll tell you one thing," Claire went on. "I am nothing like—"

"Aw, shut up!" Flossie squawked. "And put me down, you big galoot! Who do you think you are, hauling me around like a sack of potatoes?"

"Sack of feathers, more like it. What have you been eating anyhow, Miss Ross? Cat food?"

Rob tromped into what must have been the parlor at one time. Claire gaped at the appalling sight. An ornate marble fireplace belched gray smoke upward to the soot-blackened ceiling twelve feet overhead. Stacks of newspapers, magazines and advertising circulars lay moldering on the faded carpet. Antique settees and chairs that once might have been lovely leaned like old haystacks, covered with papers, clothing and cats. Everywhere—cats. Skinny and yellow eyed, they stared at Claire from atop ornate valances, an old upright piano, curvy-legged tables and mantel shelves. They peered out from under cushions and from behind Oriental pots whose foliage was long gone.

And the smell! Claire raced for a window as Rob kneed a pile of newspapers from one of the old settees and placed Flossie on it. Throwing back a velvet curtain that turned to dust in her hand, Claire reached for the sash. A cat that had been basking in the pale winter sunshine leaped to its feet, arching and hissing at her. With a gasp of surprise, she swatted the cat off the sill and jerked upward until the old window slid open a crack. Chill air rushed into the room as Claire headed for another window.

"What're you doing, girl? Trying to freeze me out of house and home?" Flossie squirmed as Rob attempted to wrap a moth-eaten afghan around her. "Hey, you're the no-good devil who stole my shotgun! And she knocked my .22 off the porch. Thieves! Robbers! Help! Somebody help me! I'm being attacked!"

"Hush now, Miss Ross," Rob ordered. He spoke over her high-pitched cries into the radio on his shoulder. "Dispatcher, this is Chief West. Send Bill Gaines over here to Ross Mansion, would you? And tell him not to turn on the bells and whistles, please. Ten-four."

"Who's Bill Gaines?" Claire asked, stepping around a heap of unwashed pots and pans on the floor.

"Paramedic. He's with the fire department. We'll let him check Miss Ross over and see if she needs to be transported to a hospital. Meanwhile, you and I can start rounding up these cats."

"No sirree, you don't!" Flossie rolled off the settee and staggered to her feet. "Nobody touches my cats! And I'm not going to a hospital, either. Where's my pistol? I'll show you, Buster Brown. Just you wait and see what I can—"

"Get back on that couch, Miss Ross," Rob commanded, depositing her on the settee a second time. "Now, stay there, and I mean it."

"What're you planning to do? Handcuff me?"

"If I have to, I sure will." He heaved out a deep breath as he turned to Claire. "What do you suggest we put the cats in?"

"I borrowed a pet carrier from my neighbor."

"*One* pet carrier?"

"Well, I didn't expect to have any help, you know. I thought I'd catch a cat or two and take them over to the shelter. Then I'd come back here and—"

"Did you call the Buffalo shelter to ask how many stray cats they can manage?"

"I didn't…think…"

"Clarence? You didn't think?" He grinned for the first time that day, his blue eyes twinkling despite the smoky pall that darkened the room. "Obviously this is a situation that calls for brainpower. Leave it to me."

With a wink, he headed for the parlor door. As he talked into his radio again, Claire heard the fire engine pull up in front of Ross Mansion. Flossie was already back on her feet and fairly spitting nails. Blocking out the sound of her great-aunt's verbal venom, Claire greeted the paramedic and the two volunteer firemen who stepped into the room. Looking as though they had entered a genuine haunted house, the three men paused, their eyes wide and their Adam's apples working to control the gag reflex.

"Uh, seems like Miss Ross has a blocked chimney over there, Bill," one of the firemen spoke up. "How about we take a look at that?" After a glance for confirmation, the two crossed the room to inspect the smoking fire. Bill picked his way toward the tiny creature who was dancing around like an imp from the bowels of Hades.

"All of you better get gone!" Flossie ranted, shaking her fists. "And leave my fire alone. Why, I'll have you know it takes me a good hour to start it every morning, and I'm not—"

"Aunt Flossie, the paramedic is here to look at your knees," Claire cut in. "You said they were broken."

"Do these knees look broken?" the older woman hissed. "Why, they could carry me to Kathmandu and back! You think I'm about to let some goggle-eyed greenhorn take a gander at my legs? Is that what you think?" Rising to her full height of just under five feet, Flossie stared at Claire. "Well, you're wrong, girl!"

"Sit down, Aunt Flossie!" Claire shouted, taking the woman by the shoulders and forcing her back onto the settee. "Sit down *now!* And if you so much as squeak, I'll tell Rob to handcuff you."

With Flossie bawling like a calf at branding time and Claire doing her level best to restrain her, Bill managed to sneak in a quick examination of the elderly woman's knees. As the paramedic retreated from the hail of verbal abuse, Rob returned to the parlor with Claire's pet carrier, the fishing net she had brought and word that the local shelter could handle ten cats and the nearby town of Bolivar would take the rest. The head of Buffalo's animal rescue was on her way with several humane traps and other equipment.

"I'm afraid you're going to have to cuff Miss Ross, Chief," Bill said, eyeing Flossie. "I got a look at her knees, and I suspect they're all right. But I'm telling you...I think we may have some other problems going on. I'd like to check her over. She may need to see a doctor."

"What's wrong?" Claire asked. Flossie was headed for the door, murmuring that she was going to fetch her pistol. "Is my aunt sick?"

"Hard to say, but I think for sure she's got...well, fleas. Maybe other things, you know."

She grimaced. "Lice?"

"Not sure. She definitely looks anemic to me. There are bruises all over her legs, but everybody knows the only place she ever goes is to the corner grocery to buy cat food and a few supplies. So I'm thinking she bumps into the furniture, maybe. Then there's the matter of her teeth. Vitamin deficiency, low iron, you name it. Her general nutritional condition looks pretty bad...."

His words drifted off at the sight of Rob West handcuffing Florence Ross to the arm of her carved mahogany settee. Her free fist pounding his broad shoulders, Flossie wailed and screeched and threatened the police chief with every manner of legal action and vengeance imaginable.

Claire could only stare in dismay. How on earth had things gotten so out of control here? Exactly who was responsible for Florence Ross? Did the state of Missouri owe her help—the Division of Family Services, Meals on

Wheels, Social Services or whatever? Were Buffalo's public servants—the police force and the city aldermen—liable for keeping an eye on their elderly and infirm residents? Should the Ross family have been looking in on their recalcitrant relative, a hermit who had unequivocally disowned all of them? Or was Aunt Flossie supposed to be capable of maintaining her own health and habitation?

The sight of the elderly woman cuffed and snarling at everyone in sight sent a curl of flame through Claire's chest. The truth of the matter was, Aunt Flossie had brought this on herself. She had alienated everyone to the point that no one wanted to go near her. For all they knew, she could have dropped dead weeks ago, and no one would have been the wiser.

Angry at her aunt, her family, the police, the state government and even herself, Claire snatched up the fishing net and dropped it over the nearest cat. A gray-striped bag of skin and bones, the animal instantly sprang to life— yowling, hissing, turning circles inside the nylon net, tangling claws and teeth and tail in a mass of freaked-out feline hysteria.

"Look at her! Look at what my niece is doing!" Flossie hollered. "She's killing Oscar!"

Oscar? This cat had a name? Struggling to keep the animal trapped, Claire reached for the pet carrier. As she tugged it toward the netted cat, a claw caught her hand and raked a line of torn flesh.

"Ouch!" she cried, tumbling backward into one of the haystacks of clothing and newspapers. The cat escaped the net in a blur of gray fur. Ears flattened against his head, Oscar made for the open window and vanished with a flick of his long tail.

"Nice try, Clarence," Rob said, reaching out to help Claire to her feet. "But I believe this is a job for two."

"Fine, then." She handed him the net. "See if you can do it."

But the cats were on to their game now. Warily eyeing the enemy, they crouched with skinny muscles coiled and sharp claws dug in, ready to bolt. The two firemen had managed to put out the fire, and Claire was forced to shut the windows in order to prevent more animals from escaping. Even with doors and windows closed, it was going to be no easy matter cornering the malnourished, flea-bitten cats.

While Rob and Claire stalked a small yellow creature that looked as cute and innocent as a baby chick, Bill attempted to examine the handcuffed Flossie. His two compatriots held her gently but firmly in place while he looked into her ears, nose, mouth and hair, then studied her arms, fingers and toes. Aunt Flossie was busy calling the poor paramedic every name in the book when Claire and Rob finally nabbed the little yellow cat. Though it fought tooth and claw, they dropped it into the pet carrier and shut the metal door.

"Animal rescue here!" a heavyset woman announced, barging into the room. She put her equipment on the floor and immediately began setting out traps. Baited with food, the small cages would capture the cats alive and unharmed.

"About time we did this," the woman offered as she

worked. "Hey, Miss Ross, how you doin' this morning? Gettin' a medical exam, I see. Good, good. We're gonna round up some of your spare kitties, take 'em over to the shelter and see that they get baths, tags, shots, worm medicine. It's just one of those things we need to do. We'll bring you back one or two, how's that? Make sure they can't start any new litters, and you can have a couple of 'em. There you go—I thought that'd cheer you up! Hey, Chief, looks like you caught one already. And is that Claire Ross? Well, I'll be jiggered. You don't look a thing like you did in high school. Remember me—Jane Henderson? I didn't think so, 'cause I was a grade or two younger, but I do recall you giving your senior assembly speech about how Buffalo was important in the Civil War. That was a good speech, and I never forgot it. Okay, let's get to work, how 'bout?"

"Hey, I helped make that presentation," Rob spoke up. "That was my project, too. Mine *and* Claire's."

Jane eyed him for a moment. "You gave a speech about Buffalo?"

"Yes, as a matter of fact, I did." He hooked his thumbs in his belt loops. "For your information, Miss Henderson, the town of Buffalo, Missouri, was founded in 1841 on Buffalo Head Prairie, which was named for a buffalo skull landmark erected by the first settler, Mark Reynolds. During the Civil War, Dallas County was pro-Union, which made it the target of many guerrilla raids. In October 1863, Confederate troops under the command of General Joseph O. Shelby burned down the county courthouse. And in

July 1864, Confederate raiders burned the Methodist church, which was being used as the courthouse."

Claire began to clap. "Well done, Chief West. I award you an A plus for excellent memory skills."

"Told you I was smart," he said. "And look at that."

They followed his pointing finger to a cat that had already ventured into one of the traps. As it leaned toward the bowl of food, the cage door fell shut.

"Voilà!" Jane Henderson cried. "Cat number two is down for the count! Tell you what. You two head on outside and see if you can catch any of 'em in the yard. I spotted a few under the porch. I'll work in here, me and Miss Ross. Huh, Miss Ross? You and me."

Flossie glared, red eyed and pinch lipped, at Jane Henderson. "You're planning to kill my cats."

"No, I ain't. Now, who's this over here in the trap? This one got a name?"

"Betsy."

Rob slipped his arm around Claire's shoulders and bent down to whisper in her ear. "Betsy? Betsy and Oscar?"

Momentarily disconcerted by the nearness of the man, Claire couldn't come up with a witty response. All she could think was that to Aunt Flossie these creatures were not wild, stray cats. They were Betsy and Oscar and who knew who else? They were her friends, her companions. Her family. And because of Claire, the old woman was handcuffed in her own house, enduring the humiliation of a medical exam by a total stranger, forced to surrender her precious privacy.

Those thoughts were running through Claire's head at

the same moment she was realizing that Rob West smelled just the way he had in high school—like shaving cream and leather and the fresh, wide outdoors. But he was closer to her now, closer than he'd ever been, and in spite of her heavy coat she could feel the steely strength in his arm around her. Near her cheek, his chest spread out like a flat plain that seemed to go on forever, and the geometric angle of his jaw grazed her temple as he hurried her out of the parlor and onto the porch.

"Whew, escaped!" he said, and his breath was warm on her skin. "Good ol' Jane. She's been wanting to catch those cats ever since she started working at the shelter, but I knew how much they meant to Miss Ross. I kept hoping I could somehow talk her into giving them up."

"Not a chance," Claire said, rubbing her bare hands together for warmth. "Rob, I think it's more than an obsession. She loves those cats."

"Maybe so, but she can't take care of them. Look at that group huddled over there near the chimney." He absently cupped Claire's hands between his and blew on them. "Mangy little things. They'll be better off with Jane. She's been fairly successful at adopting out the animals she gets. And she said she'll bring a couple of the cats back over here to keep Miss Ross company."

Claire tried to listen as he went on telling her about the local animal shelter, but somehow her mind was no longer on cats. It was on Rob West. Tall, handsome, brave, generous—and yes, even smart—Rob West. Rob West, who was holding her hands and smelled like heaven and had eyes that could make a woman quiver right down to her toes. Rob West, whom all the girls in school had had secret crushes on. Rob West, who'd quarterbacked the football team and won all those wrestling trophies. Rob West, who hated studying Missouri history and resented working with skinny Claire Ross and somehow still remembered every word of his senior assembly presentation.

But it wasn't really *that* Rob West, either. This one was ten years older and went to church and had lost his wife in a car accident. This one had become a police chief who helped plan the town Christmas parade and caught cats in a little old lady's house. Somehow all the Rob Wests were woven into a single man who was standing here in front of Claire. She knew him. And didn't know him. He was familiar. And a stranger. He was comfortably normal. And overwhelmingly, disconcertingly attractive.

"So you think we can figure out how to use that lasso thing of Jane's?" he asked, turning to Claire so that she was no longer looking at his profile but staring into his blue eyes. "If you came at the cats from one direction, and I came from the other…"

He stopped speaking and swallowed. She blinked. Dropping her hands, he shoved his own into his pockets. She moistened her lips.

"Uh, yes," she said. "That would be good. Surround them."

For a moment he didn't respond. "Did you always have those eyes? That color, I mean. Green."

"Hazel, I think."

"No, they're green."

"Well, they're the same ones I've always had. I don't wear contacts, either. Just glasses for reading." She nodded, trying to think of something else to say that made sense. "And grading papers."

"Okay." He frowned. "Because I don't remember those eyes from high school."

"You probably don't remember anything from high school." She managed the old teasing tone. "Except your speech, I guess. That was pretty impressive, by the way."

"I remember stuff, Claire. I told you I heard everything you said to me." He shifted from one foot to the other. "And I remember your hands, too. Long, thin fingers. You had pretty hands. Still do."

"Thank you." She pushed them deep into her coat pockets and wrapped them around her gloves. "Thanks for... warming them."

"Yeah, well...I guess I'd better go get that lasso thing." As though suddenly remembering he had to be somewhere, Rob turned and barreled back into the house.

Claire let out a breath. This was weird. Rob West was way out of her league. She could tease him. Scold him. Educate him. But she could not—absolutely *not*—desire him. And she knew the way her heart was beating at this moment had nothing to do with the exercise of chasing stray cats or battling Missouri's winter wind. Definitely not.

"That's far enough!" Rob gritted his teeth in concern and frustration as Claire inched her way across a tree limb toward a shivering cat. Did the woman ever listen?

"Hey, Claire, don't go any farther!" He tried again. She had insisted on being the one to go after this cat. At six foot four and a hundred pounds heavier, Rob had reluctantly agreed. "That branch is too thin, Claire. It's not safe."

"Shh!" She scowled down at him, her eyes flashing in the setting sun. They were *not* hazel. "Stop yelling at me, you nincompoop."

"Just try the lasso."

"All right, all right." Spread full-length along the branch, she gripped it with one hand and both knees as she extended the metal pole toward the cat.

Except for this wily black-and-white tomcat, the group gathered at the mansion had finally captured all the felines. Earlier in the day Rob made the welcome discovery that Florence Ross had locked all the doors to the basement and upstairs rooms, confining her living area mainly to the front parlor, the foyer and a single bathroom. After combing the house for weapons, he located the pistol and several caches of ammunition, which he confiscated. Though concerned about her reaction to the cat roundup, he removed Flossie's handcuffs.

Despite the old woman's every effort to deter them, Jane Henderson—along with Bill Gaines and the two firemen—eventually trapped all the indoor cats. About mid-afternoon, Jane and her crew stacked the humane shelter's van with ten cages. After promising to make regular checks on Flossie until they could return a couple of her cats, Jane drove away. The men begged off, saying they needed to go take showers.

That left Claire and Rob to continue the nearly impossible job of cornering the strays that lurked around the perimeter of the mansion. Climbing trees, falling through the rotting porch floor, negotiating the roof, and racing back and forth, they'd managed to nab six cats. The two indoor ones that Jane's shelter couldn't take made eight. This final tom in the old oak tree would complete their mission.

"The pole isn't long enough," Claire called down from the tree limb. "I can't reach him."

"Just come on down, then. We can leave him."

"Leave him? After all this, you want to leave him here?"

"Claire, it's one cat. Please come down. You're making me nervous."

"Rob, I'm fine—just good ol' Clarence up a tree. What do you care anyway?"

"I care, okay?"

Her face appeared over the limb a second time. Green eyes pinned him, and he felt again an unexpected jolt that zinged down his spine and settled in the pit of his stomach. What was *that* all about? She was right—it was just dorky Claire Ross up in the tree. Skinny ol' Clarence… whose curls cascaded downward like a flow of red-hot lava. Whose lips transfixed him every time she spoke. Whose peach-soft skin just about begged him to caress it.

He couldn't be looking at her this way, Rob cautioned himself. After his wife's death, he had made a conscious decision not to date again, and certainly never to remarry. The painful experience had taught him that he wasn't cut out for the job. Like the Apostle Paul, he had a God-ordained mission that transcended marriage. Rob West belonged to the people of Buffalo. He was their servant, their caretaker, their protector. In a strange sense he was wedded to a town. And quite content with the relationship, too.

Besides, women were a lot of trouble. Sherry had been unhappy with just about everything Rob did. Despite all his triumphs in high school, he learned that in his wife's eyes he appeared a total failure. Sherry hadn't wanted Rob to become a policeman. She disliked the size and condition of the only house they were able to afford after their wedding. She hated the church he had joined, and refused to attend. Most of all, she resented being married.

Though he had dated the vivacious blonde through much of high school and had believed they were in love, he belatedly discovered that Sherry had goals that went far beyond the little town of Buffalo. After graduation, she packed up and headed for college as a theater major, planning one day to move to Hollywood and try for her big break as an actress. When she found out she was pregnant with Rob's child, she reluctantly agreed to marry him, and even though she miscarried the baby, they stayed together through seven unhappy years. Sherry had regularly reminded her husband that he had killed her dreams and ruined her life. He never wanted to do that to anyone again.

"I care because I'm the police chief," he called up to the green eyes that were currently hypnotizing him into a jelly-kneed trance.

"I see," she said, still staring.

Absolutely, he could not let Claire know the effect she

was having on him. He squared his shoulders. "I can't have the newspaper printing a story about me letting the high school history teacher fall out of a tree while chasing a cat. It wouldn't look good."

"Oh, right," she said. "Well, excuse me for *not* caring about your precious reputation."

Turning away, she edged farther along the branch toward the cat. Rob swallowed as the slender limb dipped downward. The cat growled, a long guttural emanation that reverberated through the chill air. Claire stretched out the aluminum pole. The noose on its far end slipped over the cat's head. Claire tightened the loop, and the cat leaped.

"Oh, Rob!" Her arm jerked downward as the big tom's white paws and black tail flailed in midair, and she clung to the branch with one hand and her knees. "Rob, he's going to hang. I'm killing the cat."

"Let him go! Drop the pole!" Rob pulled himself onto a lower branch and started climbing the tree. "Just don't fall. Let the cat go."

"But he's caught in the noose! If I drop him, he won't be able to land on his feet. He'll get hurt."

"Forget the cat, Claire. You're the one who's going to get hurt!"

She was trying to lower herself to another branch as the cat squirmed and yowled on the end of the pole. "Help him, Rob! Move him onto a branch, and I'll try to loosen the—"

She lost her grip and toppled downward right into a large empty squirrel's nest that had been built in the crossed branches of the tree. Dead leaves flew outward in a puff of brown dust. The cat dropped to the ground and took off running with the aluminum pole still attached to the noose around his neck.

"Claire, are you okay?" Rob reached for her. The branch under him cracked. "Hang on!"

"*You* hang on!" She scrambled through the leaves to grab him. The branch snapped, and they both went down, sliding through bare limbs and snapping off twigs on their way to the ground.

"Ha! Ha!" Flossie Ross crowed through an open window as Rob rolled off Claire, who was squealing in pain. "Serves you both right! I hope you broke all your arms and legs! And your heads, too!"

Rob caught Claire's shoulders and lifted her into his lap. "Are you hurt? Is anything broken?"

"Where's the cat?"

"He's fine. I can see the pole sticking out from under the porch."

She let out a breath. "I'm okay, too. You?"

"Other than you just about scaring me to death, I'm fine."

Looking up into his eyes, she smiled. "Well, Rob West. It seems we've just completed our second project together."

He couldn't resist stroking his hand down the side of her face. "That is the last time I ever let you climb a tree."

"You can't keep me from climbing trees."

"I'm pretty good at getting what I want."

"Are you, now? Well, I certainly know what I want."

Her words rushed through him with all the force of a

dam breaking. When he spoke, his voice came out husky and breathless. "Oh, yeah? What's that?"

Hesitating, she closed her eyes for a moment. When they opened again, he saw that they had gone soft and dark. "Not much, really," she whispered. Her lower lip trembled, and she cleared her throat. "Actually, I was thinking about pizza."

He laughed. "Pizza?"

"Over at Dandy's in Bolivar." She sat up and tugged her cap back down over her ears. "They make the best mushroom-and-onion pizza I've ever tasted."

"Mushroom and onion? Whatever happened to good ol' pepperoni?"

"Fine, we'll order two." Standing, she took his hand and pulled him to his feet. "Go haul that poor cat out from under the porch, and I'll meet you at your car."

Claire was going with him to Bolivar. Rob stared after her as she headed for the open window through which her great-aunt continued to heckle them. Claire Ross was going with him to Bolivar. They would drop the cats at the shelter, and then they would drive to Dandy's and eat pizza. Just the two of them.

It would be like a date. Only, he had vowed not to date again. This was only geeky Clarence, he reminded himself. So it didn't count. Not really.

He watched her standing at the window talking to the older woman, assuring Flossie that she would drop by to check on her tomorrow and that she'd return a couple of cats to the mansion within the week. Claire's auburn curls covered her shoulders, tumbling over her green coat and down her back. Her slim hips and long legs looked just about too good to be true. As she turned to face Rob again, the setting sun flashed in her green eyes.

Maybe just one *sort-of* date wouldn't matter too much. In fact, the more he thought about it, the more it seemed like a good idea. Just two old friends having pizza together and talking. What was the harm in that?

Chapter Three

Claire wiped her fingers on a napkin and sighed as she settled back in the restaurant booth. Nothing like warm toes and a full stomach on a cold winter night. Three hours earlier, she had left Aunt Flossie still hurling insults through the open window of Ross Mansion and had driven home to shower and change out of her filthy duds into clean jeans and a forest-green sweater. Half an hour after that, Rob had picked her up in his squad car.

Back seat filled with yowling, hissing cats in small cages, they'd left Buffalo for the twenty-minute drive to the nearby town that boasted a charming courthouse square, a small Christian university and an abundance of quaint nineteenth-century homes. The manager of the Bolivar animal shelter took the cats, promising to restore them to health and try to find them good homes. And then it was pizza time.

"You only ate three slices," Rob said, starting on his fifth.

"Enough, already. I'm as stuffed as that crust."

Chewing, he grinned at her. "You always did like pizza."

Uncomfortable with the ease of his statement, she knitted her fingers together under the table. They had spent most of the evening chatting about the past—his memories of the football team, her recollections of their different teachers and their mutual reminiscences about the joint history project.

But Claire couldn't deny that it was disconcerting to have Rob West seated across from her in this dimly lit restaurant booth tonight, his blue eyes gazing into hers and his hand occasionally reaching out to touch her arm. No matter how hard she tried to convince herself otherwise, she enjoyed his company. And not just as an old high school friend. There was something about Rob that drew her. A connection, a soul-deep response, a heart yearning.

Of course, he was handsome. No female in her right mind would deny that. Just the sight of the man sent tingles dancing like snowflakes down her spine. Yet what she experienced in his presence went much deeper than mere physical attraction.

With Rob, Claire felt exactly like herself. Not like the woman she wished to become. Not like a dream image of the perfect heroine in her own life story. Just herself. Claire Ross. For some reason she couldn't quite understand, that relieved and comforted her.

And it definitely made her reconsider the man she had been so certain she ought to marry. Had she ever known Stephen as well as she knew the man across the table? Certainly she and Stephen had much in common, and Claire had admired him almost to the point of reverence. Young, highly acclaimed and well traveled, Stephen was a writer— a gifted historian whose books she had read and respected. She had been assistant curator of the museum in which he spent much of his research time, and he'd commended the accuracy of her work there.

They'd spent time together quietly discussing differing accounts of a war, or the influence of some long-dead figure, or the findings of an archaeological dig. Stephen had agreed to attend Claire's church, analyzed the sermons from start to finish and pronounced himself a believer. Though his life hadn't borne much fruit from that point forward, it had been enough for Claire.

She liked Stephen. Loved him, she'd felt sure. When he had asked her to marry him, she'd agreed, convinced that a future with the man made good sense. Their plans perfectly matched the ideal life she had dreamed up for herself in college. She and Stephen would spend their years in the serene and studious pursuit of historical accuracy. They would attend cultural events together. They would travel to the great places of the world and visit important sites. Okay, so they might not laugh much…or tease each other…or chase cats…

Claire sighed and glanced at Rob. He was nothing like her former fiancé, who had bolted off into the blue after a young admirer had made a fuss over his latest book. Stephen, it turned out, preferred hero worship to fidelity. He craved awestruck veneration over mutual respect.

Rob West, on the other hand, was steady. Authentic. And definitely a lot more fun.

He was smiling gently at her now, almost as though he was untangling and reading the web of confusing thoughts that jumbled her mind. To Claire's mortification, she realized he probably was.

"You told me your mom and dad used to bake homemade pizza every Friday night," he recalled. "That's why you didn't come to my games. Because you wanted to eat pizza with your family."

She lowered her focus to her plate. "Those were fun evenings, and my folks still do pizza night when they're in town. But I might have been giving you an excuse. I didn't go to football games because I didn't have anyone to go with. It was a culture, you know, the whole football scene. I didn't have many friends, and we weren't big on all that rah-rah stuff." She paused. "Anyway, I never have understood football."

He leaned forward, his brow furrowed. "You don't understand football? What does that mean?"

"Was I speaking a foreign language just then? No, I don't understand football. My dad never watched it on TV. He was a farm boy growing up, and he didn't care for athletics. I didn't have brothers and rarely went to the games. When I did go, I could never find the ball."

"You couldn't find the ball?"

She stared at him. "Are you going to keep repeating things? The football is brown and tiny, and it's always hidden in some burly guy's arms."

"Yeah, that burly guy is the quarterback. Me."

"How can anyone tell who's who? All the players look alike."

"They have numbers on their jersey backs. Names, too, in the pros."

She shrugged. "Anyway, it's always the same. The teams suddenly burst into action and start running around all over the field, the crowd yells, most of the players fall down and the referees throw yellow hankies everywhere."

"Flags."

"Whatever. Then the football reappears, and the whole scenario repeats itself. I never can find the ball, so what's the point?"

He sat up straight and put his slice of pizza down on the plate. Then he pointed a finger at her. "You are coming over to my house tomorrow, Claire Ross, and we're watching Sunday afternoon football."

Claire swallowed. Time alone with Rob West. This was not in her plans. Not at all. She unknitted her fingers and then knitted them back again.

"Well, I do have papers to grade."

"And I have bad guys to catch. I've got a methamphetamine ring scuttling around right under my nose, but they'll just have to wait a couple of hours to start playing cat and mouse with me again. You and I are watching a game together tomorrow. That's settled."

"Is this by order of the police chief?"

"It's an invitation."

"It sounded like a command."

"Seriously, Claire. I can't let a red-blooded American girl get by without understanding football. That's not acceptable."

"I'm not a girl." She pushed a piece of crust from one side of her plate to the other. "I'm twenty-eight, Rob. This isn't high school."

"I know that." His eyes darkened. "Are you saying you don't want to come over?"

"Would that be right—you and me alone together in your house? As my grandmother would say, 'There'd be talk among the people.' Besides, I don't care about football."

"How can you say that? You don't understand it, so you don't know how you feel about it. Look, okay? Just take a look at this."

Rob got up and came around the table. Claire barely had time to scoot over before he climbed into the booth, seating himself beside her and sliding the white paper place mat out from under her plate.

"Now, here's the thing about football," he began, pulling a pen from his jeans pocket and drawing a pattern of Xs and Os on the mat. "It's a game, but it's more than that. It's a battlefield, a test of strategy and strength. It's like that float your students are building—chess come to life."

Claire tried her best to concentrate on the place mat and the ink marks and Rob's animated explanation. With the stroke of his pen, players designated with positions such as wide receiver, tackle and linebacker marched back and forth across the white paper field. Yards and downs and penalties appeared and disappeared. Patterns formed, merged, then dispersed as the opposing teams fought to get the ball or to keep it out of the end zone. A foreign culture with its own language, football took on an unexpected mystique. The battlefield analogy resonated with the historian in Claire, and she was intrigued.

But even as she watched the drama unfold, Rob's shoulder kept inserting itself into her line of vision and disturbing her concentration. Large, solid, covered in blue denim, the mass of muscle pressed against her own shoulder—a firm reminder that the presence beside her was all man. He smelled of clean, soapy skin and shampoo. And shaving cream, of all things. Had Rob shaved before picking her up? Why? Did men normally do that sort of thing at six in the evening?

His hands kept reaching into Claire's thoughts, too. Rob had never possessed ordinary fingers, palms, thumbs. Now, ten years later, his hands looked even more amazing to her than they had in high school. They were large and tanned, with long, strong fingers and blunt nails. They had calluses and interesting small scars, and they worked in tandem with their owner's words. Rob didn't just talk—he hammered, pointed, jabbed, pounded and thumped his way through a conversation. Sitting beside him, Claire was poked and prodded, her hand regularly tapped, her wrist touched, her elbow bumped.

Under any circumstances, no one could ignore Rob West, and on this night Claire could hardly focus. Along with his big shoulder and constantly signaling hands, she had to contend with the fact that the long plane of his thigh pushed against hers, demanding her attention. His dark hair gleamed in the lamplight, and his perfect profile sent tiny butterflies circling around in her stomach. She felt as though neon lights flashed around him, blinking the word *Male*. Tall, dark, handsome male. Brave, fascinating, intelligent male. Wonderful, amazing, desirable male.

Forcing the willful word and its accompanying distress from her mind, Claire listened closely enough to manage several fairly sensible questions. Rob answered with infinite detail and more diagrams. Lots more diagrams. As the waiters began shutting down the restaurant for the night, Claire realized her place mat was covered front and back, and Rob's was looking a little like a Jackson Pollock painting.

"So a field goal is worth three points?" she asked. "Why is that?"

"Why? Who cares why?"

"There ought to be a reason."

He studied her face for a moment. "There's not a reason for everything, Claire. Sometimes things are just the way they are. Like you and me. Neither of us planned a lot of what happened in our lives."

"Random acts of circumstance and fate?" She pointed to the place mat. "Or do you believe some heavenly head coach is up there moving things around like players on a football field—planning events, maneuvering us into position, causing things to happen to us?"

"I believe the same as you. God is in control of everything, and He knows everything. But He gives us choices, too. Look at your great-aunt. Florence Ross didn't have to become a crotchety old bat, but she made decisions that molded her character. I'm sure God knew how she was going to turn out."

"I don't know, Rob. Maybe Aunt Flossie didn't choose to become so angry and bitter."

"She chose it. Babies aren't born bitter. Things happen to us, and we decide how we're going to react to them. God gave us the freedom to do what we want, and the ability to respond to whatever happens. I didn't have to get Sherry pregnant. I could have listened to my friend Claire and behaved like a gentleman. I didn't have to marry Sherry, either, but this time I was thinking about what my friend Claire would have said. She'd have told me to do the right thing and accept my responsibilities. Sherry losing our baby was one of those sorrows in life that happen—whether by God's design or the enemy's or just a confluence of events, I'm not sure. But I'm the one who chose how to respond. I imagined what my friend Claire would say—"

"You really thought of me as a friend?"

"Didn't you?" Consternation furrowed his brow. "Didn't you see me as *your* friend?"

Claire lowered her head, thinking. During most of high school she had been so lonely. Her few companions had been in the French club or the chess club or her church youth group. They had done some fun things together—silly teenage stuff. But the one person she had always been able to count on was Rob West.

He showed up for their meetings. He did his part on the project even though he clearly considered it a boring assignment. Most important, though, Rob talked to her. They rambled on and on for hours while combing through history books or painting posters or designing charts. Claire had told him everything about her family, her hopes, her dreams, her faith in Jesus Christ. And he had shared his goals and beliefs, too.

He had never been to church or had a family who deeply cared about him, and it was as if he drank in Claire's words each time she spoke of such things. He teased her and made her laugh and protected her from the taunts of anyone who dared to put her down as a skinny redhead. If friendship meant communication and support and fun, then Rob certainly had been her friend.

"I never really worked it out in my mind that way before," Claire finally said. "But yes, Rob, you were my friend. Maybe my best friend."

His mouth curved into the hint of a smile. "I like that."

"So do I. And by the way, despite not listening to my great words of wisdom as well as you should have, you turned out all right. I'm proud of you, Rob. It's wonderful that you went into law enforcement. And I'm thrilled that the aldermen appointed you chief."

"Really?" He blinked as if stunned. "I mean, that was *my* goal, but I never thought…it didn't occur to me that anyone else would…" He looked at her. "No one has ever said they were proud of me."

"Are you serious? When I heard about you being police chief, I thought, Well, what do you know? That dimwit Rob West made something of himself after all."

He chuckled. "That's not why I went after the job. I

mean, I'm glad you feel good about what I do. But I really didn't give a flip what anyone thought of me."

His expression sobered as he continued. "I should have cared more. Sherry didn't want me on the force here in Buffalo. She would have preferred that I go into business. Be a store manager or run some sort of enterprise. She wanted to live in the city. I'm talking about Los Angeles or New York, you know, where she could have pursued her acting career. But I just couldn't see myself behind a desk full-time, and I'd already made a commitment to the police academy when I found out she was pregnant. I stuck with my plan, but I understand now how selfish that must have looked to her. It caused a lot of trouble between us."

"I'm sorry, Rob."

"Well, a person makes mistakes."

Claire nodded. "You don't have to tell me that. I've made enough of my own."

"Good thing I got right with the Lord, or I'd have drowned in remorse by now. It took me a long time to forgive myself for all the stupid, selfish things I did when I was younger. But once I realized that if God—the creator of the whole universe—could forgive Rob West, then it was a done deal. God had erased my mistakes, and I'd better start letting them go, too."

Claire couldn't help leaning against his arm and resting her head on his shoulder. "That's good advice, Rob. I need to do a better job of following it myself. But I hope you don't regret choosing police work."

"I can't regret it. I know it's what I'm supposed to do.

More than anything else, I want to help people. In high school it was all about fame and glory, you know? Quarterbacking the football team, winning wrestling trophies."

"Completing an outstanding history project with your brilliant partner."

He grinned. "That, too. But after a while the hero thing got to feeling shallow. It was what Sherry wanted me for, but not what I wanted for myself. I needed some challenges that really made a difference, you know? Not just pinning some guy to the mat. Or getting a football from one end of the field to the other."

"Though that is fascinating," Claire said, holding up one of the decorated place mats.

"Yeah, all right, I confess. I still like football a lot."

"Okay...and I guess I have to confess I no longer think you're quite as dumb as a Missouri mule."

"Hey, I'm smart, Clarence Ross!" he declared. "I'm every bit as smart as you. Admit it!"

"No way!" She giggled as he grabbed her hands. "What are you going to do, Chief, handcuff me?"

"I might, so you'd better start talking, girl. Say 'Rob West is smart.'"

"No! Let go!" Laughing, she pushed on his chest as he struggled to hold her hands. "I'll never talk. Na na—you can't make me."

"No, but I can do this."

He kissed her on the lips. Hard. Once. And then again—softer, damper and sweeter.

Claire went weak as shock gave way to pleasure.

Melting against him, she drifted into the kiss, aware of nothing but the delicious pressure of his mouth against hers, the rough graze of his chin, the tightness of his hands as his fingers threaded through hers. When he pulled away, she hung breathless for a moment, suspended in the vacuum his presence had just filled so completely.

"Oh…Rob…" She leaned against the brick side of the booth, the back of her hand to her mouth. Struggling for air now, she realized she was clutching his sleeve and staring into his blue eyes and wishing with every fiber of her being that he would kiss her again.

"Excuse me, sir." A young waiter stepped up to the booth. "Umm…hey, Chief West. How are things in Buffalo?"

"Hey, Andrew." Rob turned away from Claire and cleared his throat as he shook the young man's hand. "Andrew Rodman, this is Claire Ross. Andrew's been working at Dandy's for a couple years now."

"Three years, sir. Started when I was sixteen. Now I'm a freshman in college."

"Is that right?" Rob raked a hand through his hair. "Time sure does fly. Miss Ross teaches history over at the high school in Buffalo. We had to deliver some stray cats to the humane shelter here in Bolivar and thought we'd get a bite of pizza. Nothing like Dandy's after a long day."

The waiter nodded, his eyes glancing back and forth between the police chief and the schoolteacher. "Well, I hate to bother you, Chief, but the manager asked me to tell you that we're closing down for the night."

"No problem." Rob scooted out from the booth. "We've got to get back to Buffalo anyhow."

Claire pulled on her coat and grabbed her purse and gloves. As she slid out of the booth, she felt as though she were exiting a time machine—a place where time had stopped, the past melded with the present and nothing made sense. Rob West couldn't have just kissed her. That hadn't happened. Impossible.

She didn't want a man in her life again. Not that way. Not for a long, long time. Stephen had practically abandoned her at the altar, and she wasn't about to give away her heart so soon. Certainly not to Rob West. They knew each other well, but they were just buddies. Pals.

As Rob paid the bill, Claire rooted around in her purse on the pretense of needing her lip salve. There was no way she could look at the man ever again. The whole thing was just embarrassing and silly. An accident.

He started for the door, and she hurried after him. Don't look at him, she told herself. Don't look. Don't say anything. Just get in the car.

She climbed into the squad car, and Rob shut the door behind her. They would have to talk, she realized. Two people who had just bared their souls and then kissed each other couldn't sit for twenty minutes in silence.

It felt like high school, but it wasn't. They were adults. She had been engaged. He'd been married.

But the kiss hadn't been any big deal, really. A crazy, impulsive, meaningless thing, that's all.

"So, methamphetamines," she blurted out as he started

the engine. "Wow, that's a big deal for Buffalo, isn't it? How did you learn someone was running a ring in town?"

He drove without speaking for a moment. She could see his jaw working.

"Traffic stop," he said finally. "Female ran a stop sign on the square. One of my patrolmen thought she was acting suspicious, so he searched her car. She'd hidden the meth in a pill bottle in her glove compartment. I questioned her at the station, and she told me she'd bought the drug locally. I got a few names out of her. Supposedly her suppliers."

"Did you find anything?"

"Nope. Then we started running across the stuff on a regular basis—traffic stops, domestics. Not just kids, either. Adults. Even some older folks. A real surprise. We're seeing more vandalism and petty stealing, too. The sheriff and the highway patrol are seeing the same thing. Everyone's coming up with identical information. Someone close to Buffalo or even in town has a methamphetamine lab. We just haven't found it."

Claire considered his words in silence for a moment, grateful for the passing time and the neutral topic. "I thought people usually built meth labs way out in the country."

"That's typical. Farmers keep one of the ingredients in tanks on their property—anhydrous ammonia. It's a volatile liquid fertilizer that adds nitrogen to the soil, and meth makers steal the stuff to put in their mix of cold pills and household chemicals. Also, meth has an odor, so they like to cook it in remote areas where no one can smell it. Besides that, it's explosive. They'll often rig up a lab in an old barn or an abandoned trailer. If it catches fire—*boom*. But they'll be long gone before the fire department gets there."

"Hard to believe people would take such a risk."

"Not really. Meth is profitable. It's also highly addictive. A lot of the makers are using the drug, too, so there's strong motivation. People will cook meth in the same room where their babies are sleeping and their kids are running around."

He fell quiet as they rolled into Buffalo and started toward Claire's house. "Two or three times we've found evidence of a lab." He spoke again, as if trying as hard as she had to fill the silence. "Plastic containers, hoses, burners. Personally, I think the dealers are moving around. Staying one or two jumps ahead of me."

"Like a chess game," she said. "Or football."

The corner of his mouth tilted as he braked in front of her yard. "You know, you're pretty smart, Clarence."

She managed a carefree smile as she reached for the door handle. "Well, I hope you catch them soon. And thanks for your help with the cats, Rob. I really appreciate it. I'll be over at the mansion tomorrow cleaning up, so I should have it ready by your deadline. But you're not really asking me to paint the place, are you? I mean, that's too much."

"I thought you were going to be grading papers tomorrow afternoon."

One foot on the ground, she pursed her lips for a moment. "Well, that, too. It's nearly the end of the semester, so I have to give exams and check term papers. That's why I don't have time to paint Aunt Flossie's house."

"Claire, listen. About what happened at Dandy's—"

"I enjoyed learning about football, Rob. It was fun. I'll try to watch a game one of these days. I promise." She started out of the car. "So, good night."

"Claire." His arm shot out, and he caught her hand. "About Dandy's—"

"It was okay. It was fine. Really."

"Look, I'm sorry if I—"

"You didn't. It's just that I have a lot going on. Like Aunt Flossie—I have to take care of her. And my students. The parade. Christmas. Besides, I went through all that with my fiancé, you know, so I'm not going to… to be…"

"I understand."

"Well, I'm not sure you do. Because it was awful, and I'm still angry. I'm not as far along with forgiveness and letting go as you are. I was very hurt. I don't want to be in that kind of place again. Ever. I just prefer to be alone."

"Yeah, like I would ever hurt you." He spoke under his breath. "Okay, this is Chief West signing off. And you do have to paint the outside of the mansion. At least the front."

"Rob!"

"It's in my report. Gotta follow the rules." He winked at her, though there was no sign of a twinkle in his eye. "See ya, Clarence."

* * *

Mayor Bloom waved at Rob from across the street. As a large float made of brightly colored tissue paper and chicken wire pulled to a stop between them, a gaggle of squealing, bouncy, ponytailed cheerleaders swarmed it. Crossing toward the mayor, Rob checked his uniform in the bank window. Neatly pressed black shirt and pants, patch on each shoulder, badge, name tag and collar brass with the shiny initials *BPD*—Buffalo Police Department— all in place. He'd made sure his car was washed and waxed to a high shine earlier that morning. Nothing but the best for the Christmas parade.

"How about this weather?" the mayor asked as the two men shook hands. "You couldn't ask for a better day. Sun's shining, sky's blue, temperature's hovering in the midforties."

"Just about perfect," Rob concurred.

"Mrs. Hopper's got the floats lined up in the right order. Don't know what we'd do without Dorothy. I spoke to Claire Ross a minute ago, too. She said things are all set with the parking situation at the school." He paused, eyeing Rob. "She's down there near the chess club float."

"Is that right?" Rob assessed the mayor, who appeared to be wearing the slight hint of a smirk.

"Just in case you were wondering, she's wearing a green coat."

"Aha." Rob made a point of checking his watch. "Well, I guess it's about time to get started."

"Ten minutes ought to do it. Give the cheerleaders time to get situated on the float." Bloom nodded. "Last Monday morning Jane Henderson called me about Florence Ross's cats. I hear you all had quite a time rounding 'em up. I went on over to the shelter and gave them all shots and dewormed 'em."

"I appreciate it, Mayor. That's an important community service."

"Yessir, took care of all ten cats. Did the spaying and neutering during the week. I guess you know Claire came over to the clinic on Wednesday and picked out three of 'em."

"Three cats?"

"Two for her great-aunt and one for herself. Feisty little ball of yellow fluff. She didn't tell you?"

Rob could see where this was leading. Somehow the mayor had gotten wind of the police chief and the schoolteacher spending time together, and he was not about to pass up the opportunity to pry.

"Haven't talked to her since the day of the roundup," Rob said. "I'm sure happy to hear Miss Ross has a couple of her cats back. That ought to take some of the sting out of her bite."

The mayor chuckled. "I gather she was none too pleased about the raid. Jane Henderson told me Flossie was still squalling when she left. Said she hated to leave you and Claire there to chase down the last of the cats, but you didn't seem to mind. Said you were planning to take a bunch of 'em over to Bolivar?"

"That's right."

"Ol' Dandy's sure makes good pizza. I'll tell you what."

Rob struggled to stifle his ire. One of the blessings of

small-town life—and certainly its greatest bane—was the grapevine. Everyone knew everyone else's business, or made it a point to find out. Neighbors checked on each other, and folks spent a good part of each evening sitting on the front porch watching the comings and goings of the community.

For a policeman, this was ideal. If an elderly woman fell while checking her mailbox, no more than five minutes went by before someone found her. Kids had a hard time getting into trouble, with everyone snooping over fences and craning necks to see into distant living-room windows. If someone got a new car, or dog, or wife, the whole town knew about it within the hour. Calls to the police station generally came from friends and neighbors who had spotted a problem, and Rob considered it a privilege to do his part in resolving any disturbance that marred Buffalo's quaint serenity.

But he had no desire to have his own private life strung out like grandma's wash for everyone to see and discuss. He could just about clobber Andrew Rodman right now. No doubt the young waiter at Dandy's had friends in Buffalo, and he had been eager to report that he'd seen the police chief kissing the schoolteacher.

Everyone in town probably thought they were an item, even though Rob had refrained from calling Claire all week. Not that he hadn't thought about her a lot. More than a lot.

In fact, he had driven past Florence Ross's home several times hoping to spot Claire, but it seemed she hadn't found room in her busy schedule to start painting the place.

His normal rounds took him down her street, and even though he saw her lights shining on several evenings, he never caught a glimpse of the woman herself. Even when he visited the high school to give one of his regular talks on the dangers of drug and alcohol use, he failed to see Claire.

Yet their kiss played over and over in his mind, and no matter how hard he tried to convince himself it hadn't mattered, he knew the truth. She had responded. The moment his lips touched hers, she had softened, melted, gone supple and breathless against him. She had liked it. He had, too. But they both knew better than to make anything of it. Rob didn't want to date again, and he wasn't about to get married. And Claire had left no doubt of her own feelings on the subject. She wanted nothing to do with romance.

Mayor Bloom's juicy little rumor was about to end right now, Rob decided. He opened his mouth to speak.

"There she is, her own self," Bloom said, pointing to the far end of the float. Claire had just walked around it, her auburn curls bright against the green coat. She was headed their way.

"I invited Claire to ride with us, Chief," the mayor continued. "Figured you wouldn't mind. Her on the committee to represent the schools, and all that. Jane Henderson is coming along, too. The shelter can use the community support. A lot of Mrs. Henderson's funding comes from donations, you know. Everyone's talking about Florence Ross's cats and how you all rounded them up, so I thought it might be a good idea to have the two ladies along. They can throw bubble gum. I brought a whole bucket full of it."

Before Rob could protest, the mayor pushed a plastic pail into his arms and headed for the squad car.

"Hey, my favorite kind," Claire said, stepping up to Rob and dipping her hand into the bubble-gum tub. "I didn't think you remembered."

If he could have thought of something quick and witty, he would have shot it back at her. Instead, he stared like some goggle-eyed boy as she unwrapped the chunk of pink gum and popped it into her mouth. An expression of ecstasy suffused her face, turning her cheeks an even brighter pink as her lips went moist with delight.

"Good, huh?" Rob mumbled. He handed her the tub. "The mayor wants you and Jane Henderson to throw it out the window for the kids. He bought the gum."

Her green eyes clouded for a moment. "Should be fun." She shrugged as they crossed the street toward his car. "Hey, guess what. I have a cat. Remember the first one we caught? The little yellow thing—so scruffy and wild? Turns out he's actually very quiet, and he loves to snuggle. Opie—that's his name."

Rob opened the car door for her, trying not to think about what it would feel like to cuddle up with Claire and her little cat. Trying to remember this was the Christmas parade, and he was the police chief, and...

The pink bubble that emerged between Claire's lips took him by surprise. But there it was, round and shiny and getting larger by the moment. What else could he do but—

"Robert West!" she squealed as he smacked the bubble with his palm. It popped over the tip of her nose and across the side of her cheek like a big spill of pink paint. "I can't believe you did that! Oh, great—it's stuck!"

"Gotcha, Clarence." Guffawing as loudly as he always had in high school when he popped Claire's gum, Rob strutted around to the driver's side of the squad car and climbed in. Hoo, that felt good! Nothing like busting a great big ol' bubble to lift a man's spirits.

Mayor Bloom, already seated, gaped as Claire attempted to peel the sticky film from her cheek. He gave Rob a frown and shook his head. Clearly this did not fit his mental image of two lovebirds—which pleased Rob no end. Claire was peering into the passenger's side mirror when Jane Henderson trotted up, took one look at the predicament and burst out laughing.

"Well, I'll be. You a history teacher and so sophisticated and all. Get on in, girl. I'll help you." Chuckling, she followed Claire into the back seat. "I'd have thought the gum was for the kids, but you never can tell what a grownup'll do. Every now and then I'll take it into my head to climb a tree or go wading in the creek. As a matter of fact, three girlfriends and I once ate an entire pan of brownies by ourselves. It's just one of those things."

"An entire pan?" Claire asked.

"Yep, and I'll tell you what, my husband could have throttled me the day I did that. He came into the house after work—he has a good job over at the gas station on the highway, you know—and he smelled those brownies, but there wasn't even a crumb left in the pan. Boy, he sulked about that for a week, but anyhow…girl, you have got that gum stuck all over the tip of your nose. Lean over here, and let me see if I can…well, Chief, if you'd quit jerking the car around, that sure would help."

Rob glanced in the rearview mirror as he led the parade slowly out into the street toward the downtown square. As Jane Henderson tossed a handful of bubble gum to a group of children standing on the sidewalk, Claire fastened her focus directly on him. They eyed each other for a moment, then a slow grin tiptoed across her mouth. Rolling her eyes at him, she looked away, dug her fingers into the bucket of gum and threw a bunch out the window.

"Nothing like the Christmas parade to put a body into a good mood," Jane commented. "Let me tell you what. I've been at every parade Buffalo's had since the day I was born, and that's saying something. I'm talking about home-coming parades and Easter parades—all of 'em. Yessir. It's just one of those things. But this is the first time I ever got to ride in the lead car with the mayor. Kind of puts a different perspective on things, you know, riding in the front. I've been on more than one float where you're out there in the fresh air and you can near see the whole parade one end to the other if you're up high enough. But inside this car and leading all the floats and the marching bands…well, it's just a little different is all. Not that I don't like it. I do, but you just don't quite get the whole experience…."

Unable to concentrate on Jane's running monologue despite his top speed of two miles per hour, Rob drove with one hand and waved with the other and tried to keep from glancing at Claire in the rearview mirror. Occasionally he obliged the crowd by whooping the squad car's siren in little bursts that made the kids cover their ears and shriek in delight. The mayor called out the names of friends, neighbors and colleagues as the car rolled past. And Claire, in the back seat, threw gum and attempted to blot the sticky residue on the end of her nose. And she tried her best not to look in the mirror at Rob.

Like Jane Henderson, he had been at most of Buffalo's parades, Rob realized as they approached the square with its brick courthouse and festive storefronts. The Christmas celebrations were his favorites—with the marching bands playing carols, floats depicting Christ's birth or a family reading the Bible around a living-room fireplace, and the watching crowd bundled up to their necks in coats and mufflers. But this particular parade might take first place as the all-time, number one best of show.

The reason, of course, was the red-haired, green-eyed, sticky-nosed woman in the back seat. Despite everything sensible, and every good intention in his head, Rob knew he was going to have to find a way to kiss her again. As Jane Henderson would say, it was just one of those things.

Chapter Four

"No, don't open that! Not that!" Florence Ross tottered across the room, her ratty pink bathrobe flying out behind her skinny legs and her hands clawing the air in agitation. "You stay away from there, girl. That's mine. It's my private business!"

"Okay, Aunt Flossie. Relax."

As the early-afternoon sun crept over the parlor windowsill, Claire sat back on her heels and blew out a breath of frustration. Right after the Christmas parade that morning she'd grabbed a sandwich, driven over to Ross Mansion and forced her way inside. Just getting through the front door had been a challenge. But convincing Aunt Flossie to let her throw the piles of newspapers and trash into garbage bags had been a veritable Everest.

No way would the job be finished by the time Claire had to leave that evening. Sunday was supposed to be a day of rest, but Rob West had left her with no choice but to return to the filthy old house tomorrow. Though Claire had told herself that her work on behalf of her great-aunt was something of a ministry, she would much rather have stayed home and propped up her feet. Every move she made turned into a battle of wills with the elderly woman.

"I won't open the chest," she told Flossie, "but I have to clean it. There's an inch of…well, I don't even know what this is. Newspapers cemented onto the top, old food wrappers, and here's a sweater. A blue sweater. It was probably very nice once, too. Aunt Flossie, why have you let this happen?"

"Let what happen?" Flossie grabbed what was left of the sweater—a wad of tangled yarn covered with cat hair—and pressed it against her belly. "I was living here peaceful and happy till you and that—that—"

"Rob West. He's the police chief, and it's his job to take care of people in this town. Including you."

"*Take care* of me? Stealing my guns—my only protection? Hauling off my cats? Invading my privacy? And then he ordered you to come barging in here to mess up my things. You call that helpful? You call that kind?"

"I don't like being ordered around any better than you do, Aunt Flossie. But you and I both know there's no option other than to clean this place. Besides, you've got Homer and Virgil over there to keep you company after I'm gone." The pair of mature male cats—recently neutered by Mayor Bloom, the town veterinarian—lay curled up on the hearth.

"Thanks to the fire department, your fireplace is working again," Claire reminded her aunt as her fingers ticked off the improvements. "A home-health-care nurse came over to treat your flea bites and make sure you have vitamins. I scheduled a dental appointment for you."

"Which I won't go to."

"Yes, you will, if you intend to keep the teeth you've got left. My church donated a stack of clean clothes and a nice warm winter coat."

"Which I won't wear."

"The senior center is bringing you some good food to eat instead of this awful—"

"I happen to be a connoisseur of European cuisine," Flossie huffed as Claire peeled the remains of a frozen-dinner box from the lid of the old chest. "I enjoy Italian food. French. Spanish. Even Greek."

"European cuisine? This was a TV dinner! Lasagna."

"That's Italian."

"How did you cook it?"

"I put it on the fire." She snatched the box and flipped it over her shoulder. "Oh, what do you care?"

Aunt Flossie's question reverberated through Claire. The evening she had been perched high in the old oak tree outside the mansion, she had flung that same question at Rob.

He did care, he'd told her. In his eyes she had read the depth of meaning behind the words. But instantly he'd covered the intensity of feeling with the comment that a newspaper article about her falling out of the tree could harm *his* reputation. He had hidden his emotion just as surely as he'd made certain she knew the mayor had bought the bubble gum on the day of the parade.

Rob said everything so carefully. His words insisted that Claire was simply a friend from high school—nothing more. Yet his eyes, his touch, his face…and his kiss…told a different story.

Claire studied her great-aunt, who was so wrapped up in her own miserable existence that she didn't even know how bad things had gotten. Pretending it was pleasant to live with a horde of feral cats inside a stinking, garbage-strewn house. Believing herself content. Carrying on a futile effort to convince herself that she was satisfied with her lot in life.

Was Rob doing the same thing? Was Claire? And if so, why? What was it about her that caused Rob to build walls of protection so high around his heart? He didn't seem to find her unattractive. She knew he enjoyed teasing her. He recalled their long-ago conversations, and clearly they both still enjoyed talking together.

Maybe the problem wasn't Claire. Maybe Rob was seeing someone else. Maybe—despite their unhappiness together—he was still mourning his wife. Or maybe he had made up his mind to live alone for the rest of his life.

Claire herself had chosen the latter route, hadn't she? Licking her wounds, she had decided to hide her hurt in the haven of her work, her church life, her volunteering and her little house. Now she had Opie. And she was doing her best to make it seem as if that was enough.

But it wasn't. Deep inside, under the layers of defense,

a hunger burned in her heart. A need to connect. To touch. To love and be loved. And she knew God had put it there.

It made sense, after all. God had created people in His image, created man because He Himself ached for companionship. Then He made woman so man wouldn't be alone. This urge to reach out and hold another human being was part of her fiber, Claire realized, but she had denied it by hiding away in her comfortable nest. Rob had repressed it by building a fortress around himself. And Aunt Flossie kept people at bay with her meanness and her lifestyle. But God had put His own desire for communion into each of them, and Claire knew it was time to open the door to her heart.

"I care about you, Aunt Flossie," she said softly. She laid a hand on the woman's bone-thin arm. "I really do. I don't want you to be so alone anymore. I can't be happy if you're not."

"I was happy before you came over here and ruined everything!" Flossie barked, jerking her arm away from Claire's touch. She filtered her fingers through her thin white hair and stared out the window. Her lower lip quivered a moment before she spoke again. "Once upon a time, I had it all."

"You can have it all now, too. You don't have to push everyone away. You can have friends. A family. A lovely home and a social life—"

"I don't want those things! None of 'em!" She swatted Claire on the shoulder. "Now get up. Get away from my chest. This is mine. Right here is what I had once. This—

and a lot more. I see you eyeing it. You think it's money in there, don't you? That's what you're after. I know your kind. You come in here and pretend you care about me. All you want is my money! Well, you can't have it. So there!"

"I don't want your money, Aunt Flossie, for goodness' sake."

Disgusted, Claire stood and moved away from the filthy trunk. Despite her resolve to reach out to her aunt, she could feel her ire growing again. The Christmas parade and this cleaning job would put her hours behind in grading papers. The last week of school before the winter break began this coming Monday, and she could feel the pressure mounting. There was no way she could have the house painted by Rob's deadline. The whole situation was impossible—and now Aunt Flossie was accusing her of plotting a theft.

"I have my own money," Claire told her aunt. "I'm a teacher with a salary. I bought a house and a car, *and* I have a microwave oven in which I can cook TV dinners. Why would I want your money? What good has it done you? You have to cook your meals over a smoky fire. You wear rags. Your furniture is falling apart. You have nothing, Aunt Flossie. Nothing and no one."

"I have Homer and Virgil!"

"Cats?" Claire set her hands on her hips. "There's more to this world than cats! I admit, there are times all I want to do is hide in my house with Opie. When he crawls onto my lap and starts to purr, I feel wonderful. But people should count for more than cats, Aunt Flossie."

"People? Ha!" Flossie's thin lips twisted into a sneer. "I suppose you're one of those pie-in-the-sky types who thinks people are basically good at heart. People mean well. People care about you. Well, I say that's a bunch of hooey!"

She stood there glaring at her niece, as if daring Claire to defy the accusation. "You know what? I agree with you, Aunt Flossie," Claire replied. "God created us in perfection, but Eden's gates were barred a long time ago. People are fallen and flawed and mean-spirited and ugly. We may do a little good here and there, but basically we're all the same. As rotten as that sweater you're clutching so tightly."

"You think so?"

"Yes, I do."

"Then what are you doing here trying to make nice? Get on home and rot like everybody else."

"Believe me, after today, I'd welcome that."

"You're here because you're afraid of that police chief, aren't you? Afraid he'll make you take me into your house. Afraid of what that might do to your cozy life."

"I won't deny that's what got me over here to round up the cats. But you might remember I came to see you before, Aunt Flossie. I brought you a wreath to wish you a merry Christmas. And despite the fact that you threw my gift into the mud, I came back here today because I do care about you."

"Hogwash!"

"I'm just a fallen sinner, but God forgave me. He's why I come to see you."

"Now, don't be giving me that religious claptrap, girl. I've seen your kind of people. I know about those preachers on television and how they take people's money. Bunch of hypocrites, all of you."

"Maybe so. I have plenty of flaws. But I am a Christian, Aunt Flossie, and that means I've surrendered all my ugliness and sin and failure to Jesus Christ. He took it to the cross, where He destroyed its power to control my earthly life and sentence me to hell."

"Oh, so now you're saying I'm doomed in this life and the next, are you?"

"I'm saying that the Holy Spirit lives in me, Aunt Flossie. He's whatever is good inside me. Whatever's righteous. Whatever is pure and kind and loving."

"Hush with your nonsense! There's not a good bone in your body. You took my cats. Stole 'em away from me. Left me all alone with no one but Virgil and Homer to love. Well, guess what? I don't care! I don't need anyone! I've been alone for more than fifty years—fifty years since they took away my life. Fifty years since they tried to kill me. And I was doing just fine! I've been perfectly happy, and that's all you need to know!"

Claire gazed at her great-aunt and the mounds of detritus still heaped around her. She shook her head. "Who tried to kill you? What are you talking about?"

"Them! Those no-gooders!" She hurled the old sweater to the floor. "They killed him, and they thought they killed me. Killed us both. But I fooled 'em. I'm not altogether dead yet. I have my house…and my cats…and…and…"

Flossie sank suddenly to her knees and covered her face with her hands. Her shoulders heaved, and a strangled sob escaped her mouth. Claire gazed down in confusion at the old woman. What was her aunt talking about? Who were the no-gooders? And who was this person who'd been killed? Despite the mental disorder that had led to her hoarding the cats, until now Aunt Flossie's speech had always made sense.

Claire knelt and slipped an arm around the frail shoulders. "Aunt Flossie, are you okay?"

"Do I look okay?" Fiery blue eyes flashed at Claire. "I haven't been okay for fifty years, and you want to know why? I'll tell you, Miss Nosy. Open that chest right now. Open it up. There you go. What's in it? Tell me what you see. None of that precious money you're after, is there? Hah! Told you! You're not getting a thing out of me. Not one red cent!"

Claire hesitated before prying open the lid. She reached into the wooden trunk and lifted out a stack of letters tied with a length of yellowed lace. The postmarks and stamps were Austrian. The ink, still black and clear, directed the letters to Mrs. Schmidt of Buffalo, Missouri. The return address also bore the surname Schmidt.

"Give 'em here!" Flossie cried. "You can't have those. They're mine. Let me see 'em."

She took the letters and cradled them in her lap. A prickle of excitement ran up Claire's spine. Maybe there was more to her great-aunt than met the eye. "Who wrote those letters?"

"Hans, that's who." Flossie slipped the first letter from beneath the ribbon and opened it. She read for a moment in silence. When she spoke again, her voice was wistful. "After the war, when I was barely eighteen, I joined the USO."

"The USO? I never knew about that."

"Nobody remembers it. I was the youngest of the children, and our folks had died three years before. Flu took the both of 'em, just like that. By the time the war was over, my brothers were already married and busy with their jobs and families, so they didn't pay attention to me. I was gone to Europe for two years, singing for the troops. Entertainment is all it was—just to encourage the boys. The USO trained us, you know, and off we went. Helping out. Doing our part. The fighting was done, but the soldiers were still over there. Rebuilding. Setting things in order. You don't forget your men just because the war is over."

"So you went to Austria?" Claire asked.

"I went all over—how do you suppose I learned to appreciate European cuisine? Educated my palate is what I did. And when I got to Austria, there he was. Hans Fredrik Schmidt. We met in a bakery in Salzburg. He bought me a cup of tea. He had been studying in Switzerland when Austria was annexed by Hitler, and he stayed in Switzerland, helping the resistance movement from there, until the war was over. Hans came from a good family. Very wealthy and influential, so no one suspected them of secretly aiding the Austrian resistance movement during the war. They were nice folks, took to me right off, thought I was something else. I was, too. I was pretty in those days. Had all my teeth, you know. Good figure and smart and, boy, could I sing."

Flossie hummed for a moment, her eyes misting and her face growing soft. "'Stille Nacht.' That's 'Silent Night' in German. Hans gave me a music box that played it. He would put the key in and wind it up—kind of like the apostles clock he sent over—and we'd sit together in his family's parlor and listen to it."

"Wait—an apostles clock?" Claire asked. "What in the world is that?"

"On the mantel. It doesn't work anymore. Neither does the music box over there."

Claire glanced from the ornately carved clock that she hadn't even noticed to a large, jewel-encrusted case on a nearby table she had just begun to uncover. "Hans sent you these things? After you returned to America?"

"Why not? He loved me. We were two of a kind, really, Hans and I. I'd grown up here in the mansion, and he lived in a big house, too. But we were both country people at heart. We fell in love right away. Didn't take us more than a week. He asked me to marry him, and I said yes. His family couldn't have been happier."

"You *married* Hans Schmidt?"

"Who do you think these letters came from?" Flossie fingered the envelopes gingerly, as though they might suddenly disintegrate. "He was my husband. People around here still call me Flossie Ross. Dumb sounding name. Flossie Ross, Flossie Ross—like a hissing snake. I've always hated it."

"Florence Schmidt," Claire said. "It's nice."

Flossie grinned, her face folding into the first pleasant expression Claire had ever seen on it. "Yep, that's me. Mrs. Schmidt. Frau Schmidt is how you say it in German. Anyhow, it turned out the USO didn't want married girls. Too much trouble. Hans decided I ought to come back here and set up housekeeping. So after our wedding he packed me up and sent me off. He was going to join me as soon as he got his papers together—no more than six months, we figured."

"What happened, Aunt Flossie?"

"Nothing, at first. Things ticked along as good as that clock on the mantel. I sailed back home. Hans and his folks crated up the very best of their furniture—every fine chair and rug and lamp and painting in that big house in Salzburg—and they sent it over here to me. I unpacked it all, put everything in place and went to waiting for Hans."

She smoothed her hand across the stack of letters. "He wrote me every week. Faithful as the sunrise in the morning. We had us a big plan, Hans and me. We were going to live here at the house, and pretty soon we'd bring his parents over, too. All of us together—one big happy family. There'd be plenty of room. The Schmidts wanted to leave Austria—desperate to get out, really. Folks had turned against 'em after the war, when it came out that they'd been secretly helping the resistance. 'Course, that made them heros to the Allies, and folks resented that the family had made it through the war with their house and all their belongings still safe and now were being feted by their wartime enemies."

"He never came, did he?" Claire whispered.

"One afternoon right before Christmas I got a telegram. Said there'd been an accident on a road high up in the mountains. The Alps. The car skidded on a patch of ice and plunged off a cliff. The whole family died. That was a lie, too, of course. The Schmidts had a few friends still in Salzburg, and later I got letters telling me the truth. Hans and his parents were murdered. Made it look like a car wreck, but it wasn't. They killed him."

Claire laid her hand over her aunt's. "Who did it?"

"How should I know?" The snarl returned as quickly as it had gone. "I was a twenty-year-old girl from Buffalo, Missouri. I couldn't just sail back over there and sort it all out. What did it matter, anyway? Hans was dead. All I had left of him was this." She swept her hand around the room. "Things. Furniture. And more furniture. Look at that painting over there. The frame is covered in gold leaf. You hear what I'm telling you? I got gold and silver and china and silk and velvet and ivory and more junk than you could ever put a name to. I got stuff I don't even know what it is. Musical instruments. Cooking utensils. That clock on the mantel."

"The apostles clock?"

"Back in Austria, when the hour struck, one of the twelve apostles would come out through a little door. He'd slide right over in front of the nativity scene and bow to the baby Jesus. Then he'd slide back through that other door. A different one would come out each hour. All of 'em bowed except Judas. Don't give me that look, girl. Judas did *not* bow. I saw it myself—all done with cogs and wheels and tiny chains. But I never understood how to wind the old clock. I don't know how to play that crazy-looking guitar over there, either. And I don't give a flip about these paintings. None of it means a thing to me, except that it once belonged to Hans."

"Then why don't you sell some of it, Aunt Flossie? You could take the money and move into a nice—"

"You'd like that, wouldn't you? Then you'd inherit the rest of my treasures when I'm dead and gone." Flossie glared at her niece. "Well, you can't have them! They're mine! Hans gave them to me. They were his, and I mean to protect them."

"Protect them? Aunt Flossie, you've let everything deteriorate so much that most of it is probably worthless. The clock is covered with soot. Your music box is…well, it's been buried under all those damp newspapers so long…"

Claire stretched out her hand and tugged the crusty box off the table. When she turned it upside down, she could see that the key was still in place. She tried to give it a twist, but the key wouldn't budge.

"Stuck. See? It's all worthless," Flossie said. "Just a pile of sorry old junk. And when I die, it'll all be just as worthless as I was. As Hans was. As empty and hopeless as everything in this God-forsaken world."

Claire ran a fingernail along the dirt-encrusted seam around the box's lid as she spoke. "God hasn't forsaken the world, Aunt Flossie. He's here with you. And He's with me, too."

"You think so, do you? Fool!"

"If God had abandoned you, would He have sent me here? We have each other now, Aunt Flossie. My fiancé left me feeling just as empty and hopeless as Hans left you. I never even had the chance to get married before he abandoned me. He found himself another woman—someone prettier, maybe, or smarter. Certainly she was more adoring. I don't really understand what happened. All I know is he canceled the wedding, and for a while I thought I had nothing and no one."

"You *don't* have anyone, girl. Don't kid yourself! You're alone in this world, and nobody gives two hoots about—"

The tinkling sound of the music box silenced the woman. The key had been wound to its tightest point, Claire discovered, and when she lifted the old wooden lid, it began to play. Flossie knelt at her side, and together they gazed in awe at the majestic miniature scene that unfolded before them.

Set on snowy white velvet, a group of enameled porcelain figures clustered around a tiny baby lying in a manger. On either side of the Christ child stood Mary and Joseph, clothed in brilliant blue robes and crowned with halos of clustered diamonds. As the familiar song played, a group of onlookers slowly circled the Holy Family. Shepherds knelt with heads bowed. And the magi, three of them, presented gifts—a cube of solid gold, a teardrop-shaped ruby and a square green emerald. Inside the box lid, painted angels raised their hands as they worshiped amid an array of tiny starlike diamonds embedded in the wood.

"'*Stille Nacht*,'" Flossie sang softly, her voice quavering. "'*Heilige Nacht. Alles schläft, einsam wacht…*'"

"'Round yon Virgin Mother and child,'" Claire joined in. "'Holy infant so tender and—'"

"Who's here?" Flossie broke in.

As red lights flashed on and off, Claire imagined for a moment that somehow a Christmas tree had magically appeared outside the mansion. But the heavy footsteps on the porch told her it was Rob, and the light came from his squad car.

"Ho, ho, ho! Merry Christmas," he called out, knocking on the heavy wooden door. Before Claire could respond, he appeared in the foyer and poked his head into the parlor. "Hey, Miss Ross. Afternoon, Claire. I saw your car here and thought I'd check on your progress."

Her heart beating far too heavily over the mere sight of Buffalo's police chief, Claire gave an exaggerated shrug. "We're fine, thanks. Aren't we, Aunt Flossie?"

"Better than you, you ol' scalawag!" Flossie shook her fist at Rob. "You're the scoundrel who stole my guns! Took away my cats—"

Before the old woman could scramble to her feet, Claire caught her arm. "Unless you've come here to help out, Rob West, you can just get your sorry hide back to chasing drug runners. My aunt and I are too busy to chat."

Rob's dark brows rose a fraction as his mouth curved into a smile. "As a matter of fact, I did come here to help out. Along with a few other good folks."

He turned his head, put his fingers to his lips and blew a piercing whistle. As the foyer filled with people, he continued. "After the parade, the mayor and I got to talking.

It's not too cold this afternoon, and we decided that since the fire truck was already out, maybe we could put it to good use. Several firemen, three of my patrolmen, Jane Henderson and quite a few others have come over to see what we can do for our good neighbor."

As Rob spoke, the mayor took up a position on the third step of the long staircase in the foyer and began to supervise the work. Bellowing instructions, Jane Henderson directed the cleaning crew, ordering those with brooms to start at one end of the marble floor and those with mops and buckets to follow along behind them. Two of the firemen began to work on the fireplace in the adjoining second parlor—a more formal room kept closed behind pocket doors—which primarily had been used by the Ross family for wakes. A group of women wearing rubber gloves rolled up their sleeves and began dumping into heavy-duty garbage bags the mounds of reeking newspapers that covered nearly every surface. Outside, the rest of the firemen hooked up their hoses and started spraying down the old house, washing away the accumulated grime from roof to basement.

Aunt Flossie flew into a rage. "You people get out of here!" she screeched, leaping to her feet and dancing around in a state of near hysteria. "This is my house! These are my things. You can't have 'em. Get out! Help! Where's my gun?"

Desperate to ease her aunt's panic, Claire put an arm around the old woman's shoulder and drew her close. To Claire's surprise, Flossie sagged suddenly, burying her face in her niece's embrace. "Oh, help me. Somebody please save me," she wailed.

"I'm right here," Claire murmured, leaning her cheek against the puff of fluffy white hair. "No one will hurt anything that belonged to Hans. I'll make sure of that. No one will steal it. No one wants to take your things, Aunt Flossie. I don't want anything in this house. It's all yours. Yours and your husband's."

Flossie nodded as tears rolled down her cheeks. Torn between slapping Rob and hugging him, Claire led her aunt toward the kitchen. When she pushed open the swinging door, another surprise awaited her. Expecting the large room to be filled with trash, she discovered that it must not have been occupied in years. The counters were clean, the long wood table was bare and the 1930s vintage refrigerator was still humming. Though the room was chilly and the stench from the rest of the house had permeated it, the kitchen clearly remained locked in a time capsule. After seating her aunt at the table, Claire was preparing to rummage around for tea or coffee when Rob tromped into the room bearing a large thermos.

"Hot coffee, Miss Ross?" he asked. "We've brought enough to float everybody clear to China and back. Here you go."

He set a foam cup on the table before Flossie and then faced her niece. "I hope you don't mind," he said, pouring a cup for Claire.

She rolled her eyes. "Well, now's a fine time to ask," she retorted, taking the offered coffee. "You might have checked with us before you came barging in."

"Us?"

"This is our project. Aunt Flossie's and mine."

"I hate to disagree, but I'm the one who got the ball rolling. I look at it like our Buffalo history project. It's just you and me, Clarence. And Aunt Flossie, of course."

"Just you and me? Then what are all those people doing here?"

"I brought them. Fulfilling my part of the project—like I always do."

Claire glanced down at her aunt, who was sipping gingerly at her coffee. The minute the invasion had begun, Homer and Virgil had hightailed it out to the kitchen, and both cats were now curled up at her feet. Despite the chilly room and the noise and confusion outside, it was a pleasant scene.

"You come with me," Claire said, grabbing Rob's arm and pulling him toward the door that led to the backyard. They crossed the kitchen to the darkened corner beside the old refrigerator. Claire leaned close enough that he could hear as she spoke just above a whisper.

"I'm talking to you now as the chief of police, Rob," she began. "I've just found out from Aunt Flossie that this house is filled with treasures from Austria. Most of what you see was sent here right after World War II, and its worth is probably…well, it's priceless. I'm a historian, Rob, and I'm telling you right now that nothing better disappear from this house. Your cleaning crew is not to touch one painting—not even the frames. If lemon-spray polish landed on that fragile artwork, it would—"

"Calm down, Claire."

"I'll calm down when you assure me that everything here will be treated with the utmost care and respect."

"Okay, okay." He set his hands on her shoulders. "Relax."

"Historically this is so important, Rob. Not just for my aunt and our family. It's important to Buffalo. Maybe even to the world. I don't know what she has in this house. It could be very significant. The furniture needs to be professionally restored, if at all possible. The lamps have to be taken down, and each crystal removed and washed separately. The rugs that are totally ruined can be tossed, but if there are just a few holes—"

"A few holes? The rugs are shredded and soaked in cat urine. You can smell it all the way in here! Claire, this place is a disaster. I was hoping to get those fire hoses inside and just spray everything right out the door and into a Dumpster."

"What? Are you nuts? There's a clock in the parlor that is amazing…and a music box filled with jewels…and no telling what else. It's all hers, too. It belonged to her husband—to Hans Schmidt and my aunt."

"Flossie Ross had a husband?"

"Don't call her that. We hate that dumb name."

Rob stared at her. "Claire—"

"Just don't let anything happen, Robert West. I'm counting on you to protect those valuable possessions out there."

His blue eyes searched her face. "Claire, what's going on? Do you honestly think it's worth trying to save all the junk in this house?"

"It's not junk. Not under the mess. These are my aunt's treasures. They belong to her." She took a breath, trying to collect herself. "Something happened to Aunt Flossie years ago—a terrible tragedy and loss. Her husband's death started her down this long road of mental illness, Rob."

"I told you she hadn't been born bitter."

"That's right, and I'm going to see that my aunt gets help now. If she wants to keep these things, I'm going to make sure she has them. If she chooses to sell the contents of the house, fine. I want her to be able to live in comfort and health for the rest of her life. Our family should have been caring for her all along, and from this day forward, that's what I'm going to do."

"Why, Claire? Are you doing this out of guilt? Because you don't owe—"

"No!" Claire protested vigorously. "That's not it at all. I love my aunt. I love the adventurous girl she used to be. I mourn what she could have been. And I care about who she is now. In some strange way, I see myself in her." She looked away from him. "Rob, if I keep going the way I am—refusing to share myself with people, hiding in my safe little world—I'm afraid I could become bitter and hateful just like Aunt Flossie."

"You would never—"

"You might, too, Rob." Cutting off his denial, she met his blue eyes. "I know things didn't turn out right in your marriage. I'm not sure if that's why you've changed, but I've known you long enough to see a big difference. You never used to keep people at bay. You always spoke your mind. You weren't afraid to talk about your feelings."

"I talked to *you* about how I felt. Not to everybody."

"But these days, you won't reveal your true emotions even to me. You're locked away like Rapunzel in a tower."

"Whoa, now. Wasn't Rapunzel a girl? She was the one with all that long hair, and the prince had to—"

"Robert West! Don't try to change the subject." Claire jabbed her finger at his chest. "I am being deadly serious here. My aunt got hurt, so she turned her back on people, and look what happened to her. I've been heading right down that same road…"

"Yeah, you've got your first cat already."

"This is not about cats!" she said hotly. "Quit making jokes and listen to me! You are the police chief, and you're not too dumb to hear what I'm saying. I don't want you to turn out like my aunt and me. You'd better stop pushing people away."

"All right," he said, taking her arms and pulling her close. "Is this better?"

She caught her breath as his hand slid down her back, drawing her against his chest. "Rob, I didn't mean…"

"Didn't you?"

"No, I…"

"I think you meant this," he said, brushing his lips across hers. "And this." He kissed her again, taking time to fold her in his arms and teach her lips the extent of his feelings.

Then he drew back. "Mmm, I wanted to do that again," he murmured. "Claire, listen to me."

"I see you two over there!" Flossie's high voice carried across the kitchen. "I know what you're up to!"

"Aunt Flossie, it's not what you think." Claire pulled away from Rob, eager to reassure her aunt that she had no intention of plotting with him to steal the Austrian treasures. "We were just—"

"Spoonin'! I saw the two of you. I may be a little teched in the head, but I'm not blind. Somebody fetch me some sugar and milk. This coffee is for the dogs."

Laughing, Rob nudged Claire as he passed her on his way back to the cleaning crew. "Keep on preaching at me, Clarence," he said. "I think I'm finally beginning to get your message."

Chapter Five

The moment Claire stepped out of her car she noticed the large pine wreath centered on the moonlit front door of Ross Mansion. Though its ribbon bore traces of mud, the branches were still green, and the silver bells twinkled. No tree lights glittered inside the parlor's bay window and no mistletoe hung over the door, but at least the wreath stood as a symbol of warm wishes to all who might visit the house on this chilly Christmas Eve.

Carrying the large gift she had wrapped in shiny gold paper and tied with a red satin bow, Claire stepped onto the porch. School was over for the holidays, and the townsfolk were preparing their own celebrations, yet she had no doubt many people had dropped by the mansion earlier in the day. In the past week, volunteers had repaired the steps, the porch railings and the porch floor. They had replaced broken windows, hosed down every outside wall and thoroughly scrubbed the parlor and foyer where Florence Ross

Schmidt had lived out more than fifty long and lonely years. Every afternoon that she could spare, Claire had joined the work crew, though her job had consisted primarily of calming her agitated great-aunt.

"Who is it? I hope you aren't here to sing carols at me again!" The door opened a crack, and Flossie's face appeared in the silvery light. "I've had about enough caroling to choke on, and as for fruitcake, well.... Oh, it's you. What are you doing out on a night like this, girl? Get inside quick, before you freeze to death."

Claire cast a glance at the greenery as she entered the foyer. "I see you decided to use the wreath I gave you, Aunt Flossie," she said as she made an unsuccessful attempt to hug the elderly woman. "It looks pretty."

"I'd tell you one of the other ladies hung it out there, but that'd be a lie. I did it myself. Saw it sitting over there on that table and figured I might as well put it up." She tottered toward the parlor, her cats following the hem of their owner's ratty pink bathrobe. "Bunch of old pine branches...I never did understand the point of such nonsense. But I guess it's all right. Got the fool thing out of the house, anyhow. It stank to high heaven."

"You thought the wreath smelled bad? Aunt Flossie, your house still reeks after all those cats. I'm beginning to wonder if we'll ever get rid of the odor. I imagine the curtains will have to go. And certainly what's left of the wallpaper has to come down."

"Sure, take everything. Leave me with nothing. I know that's what you want anyhow."

Smiling at the now familiar refrain, Claire set the gold-wrapped gift on a lovely mahogany table with a polished marble top. One of the volunteers had taken on the table as a special project, and tonight it fairly gleamed in the firelight that warmed the room with a golden glow. Homer and Virgil resumed their positions on a new rug that someone had bought at the local discount store, and Flossie settled into a chair that had been draped with a thick wool bedspread.

"Well, sit down, girl," the woman said. "What are you planning to do, stand there all night?"

"I just wanted to absorb everything for a moment," Claire explained as she seated herself on the edge of a settee that still needed to be reupholstered. "People have worked so hard here, Aunt Flossie. Your house is really beginning to look like a home again."

"I guess so. It's a bother, though, folks dropping by morning and night. People hammering and sawing. And you—you're the one who took away all my paintings! Why'd you do that? I liked those pictures! They're mine, and I don't want anyone to—"

"I already told you, Aunt Flossie," Claire cut in, taking her gift from the table and handing it to her aunt. "I've sent them to a preservation service for analysis. We need to find out who the artists are, when the pictures were painted and whether they're salvageable."

"Whether they're worth anything is what you mean." She cast her niece a glance of reproach. "Don't think I'm ignorant. I'm not too old to know what you're up to. You want all this for yourself!"

"Now, Aunt Flossie, we've been over this several times already." Claire pulled a sheet of paper from her purse and set it on the table beside Flossie's chair. "Here's the paper for you to sign. A lawyer in town was nice enough to draw it up. It's not a proper will—you'll have to have her help with that. But it does allow you to specify what you want to happen to the house and all its possessions after you're gone. This is a legal document, and all you have to do is fill in the blank here, and sign it."

"Well," Flossie said, crossing her arms. "Sounds like trickery to me."

"It's not a trick. After I leave, you read it over and sign it if you want. Even if you don't sign it, I won't inherit any of your possessions, Aunt Flossie. I'm not your next of kin. My parents and their siblings have that role."

"They all deeded this house over to me. It's mine."

"That's right, and you get to decide what happens to it."

Claire sighed and leaned back on the settee. How many times had she tried to explain this to her aunt? Nothing seemed to dent Flossie's certainty that everyone was out to get her. She was skeptical of the hard work that had gone into making her house fit to live in. She distrusted the people who had given so much of their time and labor without expecting anything in return. And she still believed her niece was conspiring behind her back.

Perhaps this was all part of the mental illness that had plagued Aunt Flossie since the death of her husband. Claire had made appointments with both a medical doctor and a psychiatrist in the nearby city of Springfield, but those examinations would have to wait until after the holidays. She certainly hoped the professionals could come up with a way to ease the fear and unhappiness that resided in her aunt's heart.

"Why don't you open your present, Aunt Flossie?" Claire asked. "Tonight's Christmas Eve. I wanted you to have something special."

Flossie muttered nonsensical fragments of sentences as she went to work picking at the bow. Sadness crept into Claire's heart as she watched the thin fingers plucking and pulling at the red ribbon. She had no doubt medical and psychiatric care could help her great-aunt. But Claire sensed that the greatest healing needed to occur in Aunt Flossie's soul. After more than fifty years, the woman still clung to her bitterness. She hadn't forgiven those who had murdered Hans and his parents, and the vines of hatred had choked every last fragment of kindness, hope, faith and love from her heart.

"It's a robe," Flossie said, lifting the warm blue chenille garment from the box. She frowned as she examined it. "I don't need another bathrobe. I got one already."

"Yes, but yours is—"

"How come you didn't bring me a fruitcake, like everybody else?" she sneered. "Or a chicken casserole? I've only got about fifteen fruitcakes, five casseroles and now two bathrobes! What would make you think—"

"I don't know, Aunt Flossie," Claire snapped. "I don't know what would make me think you needed something to replace that old pink rag that hangs in shreds from your shoulders. I don't know why fifteen people bothered to bake you fruitcakes. Or why five of them brought casseroles. But most of all, I don't know why you're so determined to think the worst of everyone! The people of Buffalo have reached out to you with love and generosity—"

"I'll tell you why I think the worst of everyone. You said it yourself. They're all rotten." She pushed the gift box and the robe onto the floor. "Rotten to the core."

"At least they're making an effort at kindness. They're not sitting around wallowing in their rottenness. Most of the people who have helped you are Christians, Aunt Flossie. Christians don't practice evil. They don't welcome nastiness in their lives. If they find it, they confess it, ask forgiveness for it and get back to trying to be obedient to Christ."

"Well, la-dee-da. Take your blue bathrobe and go on home. I don't need your sermons."

Rob's words to her the last time they had spoken echoed in Claire's thoughts. She did have a tendency to preach, and maybe people didn't appreciate it as much as she wished. Obviously her sermonizing had turned Rob away. Something had.

Though his last touch had been a kiss and his last words had sounded like a tease, Rob had not made any effort to contact her all week. She thought she understood why. He wasn't willing to surrender his pain. Like Aunt Flossie, he wanted to cling to whatever held his heart so tightly locked away. That was Rob's choice, and as much as Claire now wished she could change him, she knew he had to live his own life. And she would live hers.

"I promise I won't preach at you, Aunt Flossie," Claire said. "I'm through with that. I just want to tell you a little story. The end of a story, really."

"Which story? I'm in no humor for fairy tales."

"This is not a fairy tale. It's the truth." Claire picked up the blue robe and folded it as she spoke. "It's the end of my Stephen story. He was my fiancé."

"The one who jilted you? As far as I'm concerned, that's the end of the story."

Claire swallowed at her aunt's painful words before she could go on. "It's not the end of the story," she said in a low voice. "There's more, and you're going to listen to it."

"Get on with it, then," Flossie said. "I don't have all night."

"Until last week, I didn't want to let Stephen off the hook. Ever. I thought he ought to suffer for what he had done to me. His betrayal hurt me so badly that I wanted him to hurt, too."

"Serves him right."

"But then it occurred to me that my anger, resentment and bitterness wasn't hurting Stephen at all. He's having a fine time writing his books and dating whichever woman currently admires him the most. I'm the one who's been doing all the suffering—isolating myself in my little house, surrounding myself with comforts that don't really help and trying to keep well-meaning people from getting too close."

"I know you think I'm just like you," Flossie growled. "I got your point—and it is a sermon, by the way."

"No, it's not, because it has a happily-ever-after ending."

"You said it wasn't a fairy tale."

"It's a true story. You see, last week when I was over here—"

"Sure, I saw you kissing that man who stole my guns. So you're getting married. Happy wedding bells."

"Married?" Claire gasped. "I'm not marrying Rob West."

"Why not? It's obvious he's sweet on you—grabbing you and smooching you like that. And right in my kitchen, too!"

"Aunt Flossie, Rob is not sweet on me. We haven't talked for a week. There's nothing going on between us, I assure you."

"No? Hans never kissed me that way till after we were married. So if there's nothing going on, let me tell you what. You better get something going on, or the both of you will wind up like me, sitting in a big old house with nothing and nobody."

"Well, that's my point." Claire shook her head, trying to clear it. "Not my point about Rob. I'm talking about Hans and Stephen."

"Hans and Stephen? They never even knew each other. What kind of craziness are you on about now, girl?"

"I'm trying to tell you that I forgave Stephen for hurting me. I did it the other day, in my house, on my knees, by myself. I forgave him for all the pain he caused me, and I asked God to help me forgive him again when the hurt came back to haunt me. Which it does."

"You saying you want me to forgive that police chief for stealing my guns?"

Claire gave a cry of exasperation. "This is not about Rob! I'm asking you to forgive the men who killed Hans so many years ago, Aunt Flossie. Forgive Hans for dying. Forgive everyone who ever hurt you. Let it go! Get down on your knees and beg God to help you forgive everything that's ever been done to you. Just release it all. Your bitterness won't make anyone else suffer—you can only keep hurting yourself. And hurting everyone who cares for you."

Flossie sniffed as she picked at a string on her bathrobe. "Not much of a happily-ever-after ending," she said finally. "I thought I was getting invited to a wedding."

"Well, you're not. I don't need Rob West or any other man to make me happy. I like Rob. I do care about him, but I—"

"Oh, you love him. Just admit it."

"I am a contented woman with a good life. Besides, I have you to love now. You can't escape me, Aunt Flossie. I'm here for the long haul."

"Happy day." Flossie eyed her niece from under her scowl. "Well, go ahead and open your present. Might as well get it over with."

"You have a present for me? I didn't expect—"

"Yes, you did. Don't try to deny it." Flossie handed Claire a familiar box. "There. You can have that."

"A fruitcake," Claire said, gazing down at the colorful picture of nuts and candied fruit embedded in a brown cake. "Oh, thank you, Aunt Flossie. I really appreciate your sharing—"

"It's not a fruitcake! Open the lid!"

Jumping to obey, Claire lifted the lid of the fruitcake container to find the jewel-inlaid music box that Hans had given to his wife so long ago. The diamond-encrusted blue enamel sky glittered as she opened the box and watched the shepherds and kings circling the baby Jesus. As sweet music filled the room, Claire shivered at the beauty of the scene.

"Oh, Aunt Flossie," she said softly. "This is too much."

"I figured you ought to have it before one of those people who keep tramping in and out of my house decided to carry it off. You never know what folks will do. They're liable to have stripped me blind, for all I know. I bet you most of those hand-knotted Persian wool rugs are gone."

"They are gone. That's exactly right. Gone to the trash, because they were ruined by the cats." Claire rose from the settee and went to her aunt's chair. Kneeling, she slipped her arms around the frail old woman. "Thank you, Aunt Flossie. Thank you so much for thinking of me at Christmastime. I know you've been overwhelmed by…"

Claire paused at the sight of two glowing green eyes shining out from under a chair near the fire. The eyes blinked once. Then again. Claire pulled back and faced her aunt.

"Aunt Flossie, there's a cat over there."

"Homer and Virgil," Flossie said. "Right beside the fire. Their favorite place."

"Yes, but you have another cat, don't you? It's hiding under a chair behind you."

"It is? Well, poor little thing. Come here, kitty, kitty!"

Flossie turned her head and began calling in a high-pitched voice. "Come here, Sweetpea. That's her name. Sweetpea is the yellow one. Is that cat yellow?"

Claire stared at her aunt. "You mean you have more than one?"

"Just a skinny, tiger-striped fella. Came up to my back door yowling his head off last night. It was so cold. Did you ever imagine cats would like fruitcake?"

"Oh, Aunt Flossie!"

"You know, people drop their cats off right here at my house, because they figure I'll look after 'em. Sweetpea showed up today right after lunch when everybody had gone home for the day. She's so pretty. Look at her, creeping up on us like that. See her little white paws? Why, aren't you a sweet girl!"

"Aunt Flossie, you can't have these cats!" Claire said. "No wonder it still smells so horrible in here. Where's the litter box?"

"What litter box?"

"Oh, Aunt Flossie!" Rising, Claire grabbed her purse and pulled out her cell phone. In moments she had dialed the police department. Thank goodness it was Christmas Eve, and no doubt the chief would be taking the night off. At least she had one thing to be grateful for.

"Chief West here," a voice said. "What can I do for you tonight?"

Claire stared at her phone for a moment as though it had betrayed her. "It's me," she said finally.

"Claire?"

"Aunt Flossie has two more cats, Rob. I'm sorry to bother you, but—"

"I'll be right over. Try to keep them in the parlor."

Pressing off her phone, Claire stared at her aunt. The yellow cat had leaped into her lap and was curling up for a nap. How could they deny this lonely old woman her only comfort? But how could they allow the cats to return?

The place still reeked, and despite all that the volunteers had done, it would take months to restore the mansion. Claire had been upstairs only once, and she was thankful to find that the closed door had kept away the cats. But broken windows had allowed bats to take up residence, and piles of guano littered the valuable antiques. If she couldn't keep the cats out, the house would quickly return to its former state. Rob would condemn the building. And Aunt Flossie would have no choice but to move out.

"You can't keep Sweetpea," Claire said gently. She knelt beside her great-aunt. "I know you love cats, Aunt Flossie, but they need proper care. That means shots, neutering and most of all litter boxes. What happened to the box we set up for Homer and Virgil?"

"Oh, it's over there where you put it. Someplace... I don't know."

"It has to be kept clean, Aunt Flossie, or the cats will stop using it."

"I don't care what they do. Let 'em have the run of the place." She looked up and squinted at the red lights flashing outside. "What now? Wonderful, it's your boyfriend come to call. Next thing you know, you'll be spooning right here in the parlor."

"Aunt Flossie, we were not—"

"That thief. See if you can get him to give me back my guns." She stroked the yellow cat's head. "Ain't that right, Sweetpea? We need to have some protection from all those do-gooders who keep barging into our house."

Claire stood as Rob stepped into the parlor. "I didn't think you'd be working tonight," she said.

"Figured I'd let the other boys have the evening off. They've all got families." He shrugged as he turned his attention to Flossie. "Evening, Miss Ross. Who's that you got there in your lap?"

"Sweetpea." Flossie glared at him. "Thief!"

Rob chuckled. "You can have your guns back, Miss Ross, as long as you agree not to fire them inside city limits again."

"What good is that? How do you suppose those Union soldiers would have fared if they hadn't had their guns when the Confederates attacked the town?"

"They didn't fare too well even with their guns, ma'am. The Rebs burned down the courthouse and the Methodist church anyhow." Rob winked at Claire. "Isn't that right, Miss Ross?"

Claire couldn't help smiling at his reference to their project. "That's right, Chief West."

"Oh, now it starts," Flossie said. "The two of you moonin' over each other like a pair of doves. Coo... coo...coo. Cuckoo is what you are. Well, get on with your courtin' and leave me—"

"Aunt Flossie," Claire cut in quickly, "Chief West has come out here to take Sweetpea and the tiger-striped cat to the shelter."

"Felix is his name, and you can't have either one of 'em. They're mine. They came to live with me."

"We'll figure out what we can do about Sweetpea and Felix after we get them over to the shelter," Rob said. "Jane Henderson and Dr. Bloom both need to have a look at them. Let me see that little gal there. Come here, Sweetpea."

Rob lifted the kitten into his arms and ran his hand down the small creature's scraggly fur. Claire's shoulders sagged in relief. Reaching out, she stroked her fingers over the poor animal.

"She put fruitcake out for them," Claire whispered. "There's no telling how many more will wander over here. Rob, I just don't know what to do. Can you smell that awful odor? Already the cats have stopped using the—"

"Wait a second!" Stiffening, he lifted his head and breathed in. "Here, you'd better take this cat."

"Rob? What's going on?"

"Dispatcher," he said into his shoulder radio. "This is Chief West. I'm at Ross Mansion. I'm going to need all the backup I can get. Send my men over here—everyone—and alert the highway patrol and the sheriff."

"Backup?" Claire said. "So far it's just two cats, Rob. You're not going to need the highway patrol and the sheriff."

"That smell, Claire. It's not just cats. There's another odor underlying it." He studied her for a moment. "You smell that?"

"It smells like just cats to me."

"It's not. That's the odor of a methamphetamine lab."

While Rob watched out the window for his backup to arrive, Claire calmly kept her great-aunt talking, carrying on a conversation about the past. Though he knew it could be dangerous to remain in the house, he had no desire to alert the methamphetamine manufacturers that something was up. If his suspicions were correct, they had grown accustomed to seeing his squad car parked outside, and they had chosen to brazenly continue their illicit activities right under the noses of Buffalo's good citizens. A few minutes ago Flossie had given Rob her permission for the authorities to conduct a search, and as long as she kept up her chatter, he hoped no one would suspect what was about to occur.

Castigating himself for failing to note the odor earlier, Rob wondered where the lab was hidden. It could be in a residence nearby. Or the carriage house on the mansion's grounds. Or possibly somewhere in the old building itself. The basement, perhaps? Or the attic? It was clever of the criminals to choose this spot. The building was centrally located, yet the odor of Flossie's cats masked the smell of the drug dealers' operation.

As Flossie began some sort of harangue about fruit-cake, Rob's assistant chief, his corporal and three of his five patrolmen pulled up to the mansion all at the same time and all within five minutes of his call to the dispatcher. Good. His first priority now was to get the two women to safety and secure the site. After that, his men could scour the area for the source of the meth odor.

"Claire," he said, crossing the parlor to the fire. He slipped his arm around her and pulled her aside. "I want you and your aunt to leave the house now. I know how you feel about this, but can I ask you to take Miss Ross home with you? I promise you we'll have her back in here by morning. You won't have to put up with—"

"Rob, it's fine," Claire said. "I'm happy to take Aunt Flossie home with me."

"I ain't goin' nowhere!" Flossie squawked. "This is my house, and I'll be hog-tied and strung up before I let you run me out of it."

"Listen, Aunt Flossie," Rob said, switching to the more comforting name her niece used. "Someplace near your house, people have set up a laboratory. They're making a drug called methamphetamine. It's dangerous, because it can explode. I don't know if the meth makers are inside the mansion or in one of the houses surrounding you. But if they're near enough to smell, they're too close. Now, I want you to go home with Claire until we take care of this problem. Do you understand?"

"No, I do not! This is my house, my property! What are those policemen doing here? Hey!"

"Stop hollering," Claire said, putting a finger to her lips. She helped the elderly woman from her chair and edged her toward the parlor door. "Come on, Aunt Flossie. You and I are leaving now. We'll go to my house, drink some hot chocolate and listen to Christmas carols."

"Not that!" Flossie cried. "Not carols!"

Rob shook his head as he strode out of the room just ahead of the women. Lifting up a quick prayer of gratitude, he marveled for a moment at the change in Claire. Just a few weeks before, she had flatly refused to ever let her aunt inside her own home. Now she welcomed the opportunity. Claire had accused Rob of barricading his own heart, and he couldn't deny it. But could he really let down his walls? And if he did, what would happen?

Needing to confer with his men, he trotted across the barren lawn toward the gathered squad cars. The Buffalo patrolmen had run this exercise so many times—and always in vain—that he knew he would barely need to give orders. They had the drill down pat, and finally it looked as if they were about to catch the bad guys.

As Rob greeted his men, the sheriff and several deputies arrived on the scene at the same moment as Buffalo's other two patrolmen. Under Rob's direction and with the sheriff's concurrence, the deputies formed a perimeter around the mansion and the surrounding homes, covering streets, alleyways and yards to prevent anyone escaping. Three highway patrol units pulled up as Rob ordered his own men to proceed toward the house.

He opened the door of his squad car for protection and was watching the operation unfold when suddenly he saw Claire Ross appear in the mansion's front doorway. Pulling on her great-aunt's arm, she was doing her best to urge the elderly woman out onto the porch. Flossie would have none of it. Wrapped up in a blue bathrobe, she held one cat against her chest and kept reaching for another, finally breaking loose from her niece and disappearing back into the house.

Alarm prickling down his spine, Rob called to the sheriff across the driveway. "In the foyer! It's the homeowner and her niece. I thought they'd gotten out."

"I'll cover you," the sheriff replied.

At that moment one of Rob's men ran up. "We found 'em, sir," he panted. "They're in the basement. Seems they've been coming and going through a window hidden behind some yews. We can see 'em in there—looks like they're already breaking down the lab. I think they're on to us, Chief."

"How many?"

"Six, at least. Five males and a female."

Rob spoke into his radio, narrowing the deputies' perimeter to the yard surrounding the mansion. Then he headed for the front door. As his foot hit the foyer's marble floor, Claire looked up, her face ashen. "I can't get Aunt Flossie out, Rob."

"Leave her to me." Rob strode into the parlor where Claire's great-aunt was seated by the fire again. Two cats were just settling onto her lap as he stepped up, scooped the scrawny woman into his arms and swung around to the door.

"Florence Ross, you are a mean old lady," he said as he carried her out into the foyer. "Mean and selfish. And if you don't start cooperating, I'm going to have to—"

A loud bang resonated through the house. Flossie stiffened in Rob's arms. "It's the basement door!" she hollered. "Someone's breaking in! They'll steal my things! I'm being robbed! Call the police!"

"Where's the basement door?" Rob demanded.

"In the kitchen!"

Setting Flossie back on her feet, Rob rushed the elderly woman and her niece out the front door. As he drew his gun, he intercepted three men who had just exited the kitchen and were hightailing it up the long curved staircase leading to the second floor of the mansion.

"I need backup inside," Rob shouted into his radio as he pursued the men up the steps. "Stop! You three, stop now. Get on the ground!"

Ignoring his orders, they raced up the staircase. Rob knew if they made it into the honeycomb of rooms up there, they would have an easier time eluding pursuers. But bless Aunt Flossie's cold little heart, he thought as the men hit the top landing—she had locked the door to the upper floor.

Trapped, the men had no choice but to turn around and raise their hands in surrender. Two sheriff's deputies pounded up the staircase right behind Rob. In moments, they'd handcuffed the three suspects and led them back down the stairs.

Outside, Rob found that the rest of the methamphetamine makers had been captured, as well. One of the men had cut his arm while trying to escape through a broken window, so an ambulance was on its way. The others— cuffed and shackled—sat staring at the ground as an officer recited their Miranda rights.

"Chief West, I've already called for the haz-mat crew,"

one of the highway patrolmen spoke up. "I think we should secure the building and stay out of it until they get here."

Rob nodded. The hazardous materials experts would know how to safely disassemble the lab in the basement.

"There were two women in the house," he said, his heart hammering. "Did they…"

"They're out, Chief," his assistant said. "Miss Ross and that redheaded teacher over at the high school? They exited the building a couple minutes ago. The redhead took Miss Ross off in her car. Told us they'd both spend the night at her house."

Thanking God for Claire's safety—and for Aunt Flossie's—Rob felt the knots in his stomach loosen as he studied the growing crowd of neighbors and other onlookers. He would need to unroll crime-scene tape and set up barricades to keep folks back. What a way to spend Christmas Eve! It looked as if he and his men wouldn't get home until nearly dawn.

"Say, that teacher sure is pretty," the assistant chief spoke up again. "The redhead."

"Her name is Claire," Rob said. "Claire Ross."

"Was she the one you took to Dandy's in Bolivar the other night? I heard you two had a good time."

Rob sighed. People were elbowing each other as the ambulance pulled up to the mansion. Another night in Buffalo, Missouri, where minding one's own business was clearly an alien concept.

Chapter Six

"Not enough singing, if you want my opinion." Florence Ross Schmidt allowed her niece to assist her down the church steps following the community Christmas service. Wearing one of Claire's dresses—Flossie had selected a pink satin print—and high heels only a tad too large, she clutched a black purse between her gloved hands.

"Not enough singing, Aunt Flossie?" Claire asked in wonder. "Only yesterday you were complaining about the carolers who had been to your door."

"It's one thing when people come knocking at all hours. And it's quite another when you get to exercise your own vocal chords."

"You do have a pretty voice. I can see why you enjoy singing." Claire scanned the crowd one last time, but Rob was not among the cheery congregation. She hoped he was all right.

Before the service began, the pews had been abuzz with talk of the previous night's raid. Methamphetamine makers in *our* town, people said, shaking their heads in disbelief. Four men and two women were caught in the attic of Ross Mansion. No, it was six men and one woman, someone clarified. Five men but no women, another explained, and they were in the basement.

The whole town had gone out to watch the excitement, it seemed to Claire. People had been up till all hours, peering over the barricades as the officials conducted their investigation and the hazardous materials crew disassembled the lab. Claire felt thankful it was all over. Now the mansion would be safe, and the odor certainly lessened.

"I always was a good singer," Flossie told her niece as they headed toward the parking lot. "Why do you think the USO took me without a squawk? I could really belt 'em out in my day. Hans used to beg me to sing for him. I learned a lot of his favorites in German."

They walked in silence for a moment, Claire reflecting on her great-aunt's loss and the enormous changes that had been imposed on the elderly woman in the past few weeks. Would Claire have fared as well if her world had been turned upside down?

Flossie had put up a mighty fuss until the moment Rob finally rushed her out of the mansion the night before. After that she had done an about-face. Once inside Claire's little bungalow, she warmed immediately to the rescued kitten, Opie. Meekly accepting the order to take a bath, she had sat for nearly an hour in a tubful of bubbles. Then she emerged in her new blue bathrobe and immediately adopted as her own a rocking chair by the fireplace. Together, the two women drank hot chocolate beside the little Christmas tree while Flossie crooned carols.

Claire had expected a monumental storm over the prospect of attending church the following morning, but her aunt actually displayed a certain girlish eagerness as she selected a dress and shoes. She allowed Claire to curl and style her white wisps, and then they ate breakfast like a civilized guest and her hostess.

"Hans could sing, too, and we made a nice duo." Flossie continued the conversation. Then she shrugged and flipped her hand as if to brush away the past. "But that was all in the old days. What's gone is gone."

"It's okay to keep your memories, Aunt Flossie," Claire said gently as she reached for the car door handle. "Just don't try to live in the past."

"Preaching again." Flossie settled into the passenger seat. "Preach, preach, preach."

As much as she enjoyed the changes in her aunt, Claire would be relieved to send the elderly woman back to the mansion in a few days. Maybe Claire was more cut out for the single life than she'd wanted to admit. Rob certainly had made up his mind in that direction. Despite kissing her—nothing more than a teasing impulse, she realized now—he showed no inclination toward forming any sort of relationship with her. Not even a real friendship. He never called, nor did she. They enjoyed talking when their paths crossed, but she felt certain it would happen rarely now that Flossie was under proper care.

Opening the driver's door, she climbed in and settled her purse beside her. "The turkey I put in the oven is going to taste good," she told her aunt. "I'll mash some potatoes and fix us a salad, too. Will you help me set the table?"

Hands folded, Flossie was staring out the window ahead. "That table you have is nice," she said. "In fact, I like the little house. Two bedrooms. Just right. I think we oughtta swap."

Key halfway to the ignition, Claire paused. "Swap?"

"Trade houses, girl, what do you think? You've had your eye on my place all along anyhow, and I've taken a shine to yours. Why don't you just take the old heap—and all that junk inside it, too. Junk, junk, junk. I don't know what half of it is anyhow, and I sure don't need it."

"But, Aunt Flossie, the mansion belongs to you." The thought of surrendering her precious little nest sent a stab of panic into Claire's heart. "I really do love my home, and you certainly belong in the mansion. I'd be happy to help you fix it up. Some of the furniture is still very nice, and we could make you a little bedroom area, along with a sitting room and a dining table. Besides, you don't want to live without all the things you said meant so much. The paintings will be back soon, and we'll bring some nice carpets down from the upstairs rooms, and the apostles' clock—"

"That old thing doesn't work worth a hoot. Who wants all those apostles sliding around and bowing every hour, anyhow? Not me." She waved her hand in dismissal. "Nope, it's yours. I prefer that nice clock hanging on your wall. Just a dial and a pair of hands. Easy to read, and no Judas popping out every twelve hours to scare the pants off a person."

Though the idea of preserving the mansion definitely excited Claire, she had no intention of surrendering her home to her great-aunt. If she had to live all alone in that imposing space, she might turn into a cat hoarder herself.

"Uh-oh, here he comes." Flossie broke in to her niece's thoughts. "Your boyfriend. Here to grab you and start smooching you again right in front of God and the whole town. Lord have mercy upon us."

"Aunt Flossie, Rob is not my boyfriend," Claire hissed as the man strode up to her car. "And if you so much as—"

"Merry Christmas," the police chief said, peering through the window Claire had just rolled down. "How are my two favorite Rosses this morning?"

"My proper name is Mrs. Schmidt," Flossie informed him, tilting her nose in the air. "I'd prefer to be addressed as such in the future, Mr. West."

Rob's blue eyes turned on Claire, and his brows rose. "Well, it looks like we're off to a good start."

"We are, actually," Claire said. "The church service was lovely—"

"Not enough singing," Flossie put in.

"And I have a turkey in the oven."

"I sure hope your bird can wait a few minutes." Rob

opened her door. "Claire, will you and Mrs. Schmidt please come with me? The three of us need to pay a little visit."

"A visit?" Claire protested. "But I—"

"Oh, hush your yapping. No one likes being around a griping woman." Flossie settled Claire's purse strap over her arm as she stepped back onto the parking lot. "I wish you'd assist me to your car, Chief West. These heels just aren't made for winter sidewalks."

Turning a shoe from side to side as if to show off her ankle, Flossie was actually flirting with the police chief, Claire realized. What had come over the woman? Had getting out of the mansion done that much for her? Or had Flossie actually listened to her niece for once and forgiven those who had hurt her in the past?

"We're swapping houses," she informed Rob as he escorted her to his car.

Wearing a bulky dark blue sweater and a pair of jeans that fitted him far too well for Claire's comfort, he arched an eyebrow as he looked over his shoulder at her. "Swapping?"

"I'm moving into her house," Flossie explained, "and she'll take the mansion. It's what she's always wanted, you know. Had her eye on my stuff all along. But I don't care! Let her have it. Just a pile of junk anyhow. I'll take Homer and Virgil and move into the smaller place. Sacrifices, you understand. They're part of life."

"Hmm, this is an interesting development," Rob said, studying Claire's face across the top of the car as he settled her great-aunt into the front seat. "It'll make the museum plan easier anyhow, I'll give it that much."

"What museum plan?" Claire asked as she slid into the back seat. "And by the way, I have *not* agreed to swap houses with you, Aunt Flossie. That's your idea, and I... What museum plan?"

Rob smiled as he started the car and pulled out into the street. "The Buffalo Historical Museum. Mayor Bloom and I have been discussing it for quite some time. I told him how significant Buffalo was during the Civil War. It was pro-Union, you know, Claire."

Irked at his teasing, she clenched her fists. "I'm aware of that, Rob. What do you mean about the Buffalo Historical Museum?"

"You see, Mrs. Schmidt, Confederates burned down the courthouse and the old Methodist church," he went on. "And then there's all that important history connected to the railroad. A spur was supposed to come into Buffalo, but it was never built. In anticipation of the increased opportunity, though, people moved here and started businesses and built big houses. Which is why Ross Mansion would make a perfect museum."

"It's a museum, all right," Flossie said. "Full of dead dreams, dead hopes, emptiness. You can do whatever you like with it. I don't ever want to set foot in the place again."

"You'll need to go inside at least once more," Rob said as he pulled to a stop in front of the big old house. "I don't think you'll mind this time."

"But I thought we were going to go calling on some-one," Flossie protested. "I was hoping for a slice of pecan pie. That's my favorite. I don't know why nobody asked what I liked before they started bringing me all those fruit-cakes."

As Flossie went off on a tangent, Claire clambered out of the car and made a beeline for Rob. "Do not tease me, Robert West," she said, catching handfuls of his sweater. "Does the mayor really like the idea of a museum?"

"Sure, and the aldermen, too. Especially if Miss Ross—Mrs. Schmidt—would allow Ross Mansion to house it."

"Are you serious? How did this happen?" Claire accompanied Rob as he headed for the porch. "This is what I've been dreaming about! When I first came back to town, I spoke to the mayor and several of the aldermen, but none of them showed much interest. What did you do, Rob?"

Laughing, he slipped his arm around her as Flossie stepped into the foyer. "I just mentioned it last night while we were all standing around. Mayor Bloom was out in the crowd, of course, along with most of the aldermen. I told them what you'd said about all the valuable pieces inside the house, about the things from Austria, and about how much a museum might mean not only to your family but to the whole town."

"Oh, Rob…"

"Mercy sakes!" Flossie screeched. "Look at it! Look what they've done!"

Claire stepped into the parlor and gasped. A wonderland of twinkling white lights, chandeliers draped in gold ribbon, swags of pine branches and the fragrance of sweet cinnamon and nutmeg, the room fairly cried out, "Merry Christmas!" A fire crackled on the grate, while Homer and Virgil stretched out before it like a pair of indolent sultans.

"My kitties!" Flossie cried, tottering over to them in Claire's high heels. "Aw, look at you pretty cats! I bet you feel happy today, don't you?"

As her aunt knelt to stroke the pets, Claire felt Rob's arms come around her. Standing behind her, he whispered in her ear, "You missed the best part." Then he turned her toward the bay window, where a huge tree towered to the ceiling. Covered in colorful ornaments, ribbons and gold garland, it glittered with hundreds of tiny white lights. "Jane Henderson and some of the ladies cooked up this surprise last night. Jane and Mrs. Bloom headed the committee. The investigation was complete, so I gave my permission and helped them bring in the tree. They came over here before church to set everything up."

"I can't believe it," Claire whispered back. "All the work they'd already done on the house...and now this room... and the museum, too. Rob, why?"

"I think you infected the whole town with the Christmas spirit."

"Me? I was just trying to keep you from throwing Aunt Flossie out."

"So she wouldn't have to live with you."

Reveling in the warmth of his arms around her, Claire leaned her head back against Rob's chest. Though she knew she shouldn't enjoy his presence so much, she couldn't help herself. Maybe this was all she would have of him— a few hugs and the occasional impulsive kiss—but she would drink it in like cold water on a hot day.

"I can't deny it," she said. "I had the worst attitude."

"God can take the worst and turn it into the best. You taught me that a long time ago. And you showed the rest of the town by tackling the whole Flossie Ross problem head-on."

"Don't call her that, remember? Flossie Ross—we hate that name."

He chuckled. "You two are quite a pair. I think she'll be willing to move back in once we fix a few rooms upstairs just for her. With the museum on the main level, she'll have plenty of company, and no one will let a cat through the front door."

Claire closed her eyes, soaking up his presence and thanking God for miracles large and small. "You've been wrong about only one thing, Rob," she murmured. Fighting tears, she forced herself to speak her heart. "You said the tree was the best part. It's not. This is."

Silent behind her, he tightened his arms around her waist and rested his cheek against her head. Carrying a cat, Flossie walked across to the table that held the jeweled music box. When she lifted the lid, the notes of the hymn drifted through the room.

"'Silent night,'" Flossie began to sing. "'Holy night. All is calm, all is bright…'"

"Claire, you challenged me to be more open with people," Rob said in a low voice. "To be more open with you. I've watched you change as you opened up to your aunt. And even Flossie changed as she finally let you in. The thing about me is just that I—"

"It's okay, Rob. You don't have to say anything."

"I want to talk. But I don't know if you'll want to hear what I have to say."

Claire struggled to hold back the tears that threatened. "Go ahead and be honest. I'm your friend, Rob."

"You're my friend, that's true. But…" He let out a breath that was warm against her ear. "But, Claire, I love you. I've loved you from the moment I walked into the gym and Mr. Jackson handed me the name of my partner and I saw it was you—a skinny freshman with red hair that stuck out in strange directions and a sharp tongue and a heart that was bigger than any I'd ever known. I loved you way back then, but I was too thick to admit it—okay, I was as dumb as a Missouri mule and twice as ornery. Doing things my own way took me down the wrong path, just as you said it would. But God saved me and brought me to Him and gave me a reason to live again. And then He put you back into my life. Claire, I know you just see me as a friend, and you've been through all that pain in the past, and you've worked hard to make a new life for yourself, but—"

"But if you don't kiss me right now, Robert West," she

said, turning in his embrace and throwing her arms around his neck, "I don't know what I'll do."

Without waiting, she stood on tiptoe and kissed him with every ounce of feeling that had been building inside her for so long. "Oh, Rob, I love you, too. I love you so much I'm about to burst with it!"

"Claire, are you sure?"

"Of course I'm sure. You know I always speak my mind."

"Then I want you to have my heart," he said softly. "Just take it and hold it and keep it safe forever. Will you do that?"

She searched his eyes. "Forever?"

"I want you to be my wife, Claire. I know it's sudden, and I don't mind if you take your time—"

"Yes!" she cried, the tears at last spilling down her cheeks. "Yes, I want to be your wife, now, always, forever!"

With a burst of laughter he caught her up in his arms and swung her around. "Do you mean that? Oh, girl, I've been going crazy over you!"

"Rob, this is too much! I can't believe—"

"Here we go again," Flossie cut in as she hobbled across the room, shaking a finger at them. "Spooning right here in public. Kissing and giggling and whatnot. Let me tell you something, young man. You'd better have honest intentions toward my niece. She's a fine girl, and I mean to protect her from the likes of scalawags and scoundrels."

Claire and Rob stared at Flossie for a moment, and then they swept her into their hug. As the three turned around and around in the parlor, the music box mirrored their movement—shepherds and kings circling the holy infant, so tender and mild. Through Him, promises made would be kept. Miracles begun would end in completion. What was broken would be made whole. And one day, the whole world would sleep in heavenly peace…sleep in heavenly peace.

* * * * *

CHRISTMAS MOON

Gail Gaymer Martin

"'Twas in the moon of wintertime
When all the birds had fled,
That God, the Lord of all on the earth,
Sent angel choirs instead.
Before their light the stars grew dim,
And wond'ring hunters heard the hymn:
Jesus your king is born!"
—Jean de Brebeuf, traditional carol

To my husband, Bob, who has given me more than I could ever return. He is my support, my cheerleader, my housekeeper, my cook, my laughter, my love. Thank you, Lord, for this wonderful gift.

Chapter One

"Rose...I want you to marry me."

Rose Danby's spoon clanged into the sink as she spun around to face her employer. She searched his face, expecting to see a grin, but he looked serious. He was handling the joke with the skill of a stand-up comedian.

"So...what's the punch line?" Rose asked.

Paul Stewart faltered. "It's not a joke. I was thinking that—"

"It's not a joke?" She felt her forehead rumple like a washboard. Not that she wouldn't want to marry a man as kind and handsome as her employer, but she was his twins' nanny. "What do you mean it's not a joke?"

His gaze searched hers. "I'm sorry. I shocked you." He moved closer. "It just makes sense."

"It makes sense to you, maybe, but I don't get it."

He glanced over his shoulder before refocusing on her. "Are the twins sleeping?"

She nodded. "They went to bed about an hour ago."

A relieved look settled on his face, and he pulled out a kitchen chair. "Could we sit and talk?"

Talk? She felt her legs tremble and realized sitting was a wise move. Before she took a step, the teakettle whistled. "How about a cup of tea…while we chat?"

Without waiting for an answer, she moved to the stove and pulled the water from the burner. Talk? What more could he say after his "I want you to marry me" line?

Rose made the tea with as much speed as her shaking hands could manage, then set a mug in front of him and sat across from him with her own. "What's this about?"

He raised his focus from the cup to her face. "I've been asked to take a transfer. Told is more accurate."

"Transfer?" Her world spun out of control. What would she do? She had taken this position more than a year ago after a romantic fiasco. She wasn't ready to find another job. "You mean transferred out of L.A.?"

He nodded, then refocused on the tea.

"Transferred to where?"

"Minnesota."

She felt her breath escape. "Minnesota?"

He inched his gaze upward. "To Little Cloud."

"But why? I don't understand."

"One of our branches is having serious problems. They'll give me two years to troubleshoot or close the place." He rubbed the back of his neck, then shook his head slowly. "That's why I need you. The kids need you."

The kids. What would life be like without his four-year-old twins? Ice edged through her veins. Though she had a huge challenge with Paul's daughter, Kayla, Rose loved the children. Kayla had been born a quiet child, and her brother, Colin, had taken over for her. She mainly communicated through Colin and occasionally her father. But Rose had finally made progress. What would happen if they moved away? Kayla needed her. They both did, and she needed them, but... Her thoughts were a jumble, but one thing was clear.

"I can't marry you, Paul."

Though she spoke the words, the vision of being in Paul's arms rose in her mind. She had dreamed it before, then scolded herself for being so foolish. She was the nanny. The dinner maker. Even the thought of another employer-employee romance made her recoil.

His brown eyes sparked with concern. "But I can't go without you, Rose. I can't find someone to care for my kids and handle a floundering corporation without help."

"You didn't ask me to help. You asked me to marry you. They're different." A deep sigh escaped her. She longed to say yes, but she was a Christian—a woman who knew love and commitment were what the Lord expected for marriage.

She shook her head. "I can't leave Los Angeles, and I can't marry someone who doesn't love me." Old memories tore through her and left her reeling.

"I thought you loved the kids."

"You didn't ask me to marry the kids. I love them with all my heart. The thought of losing them kills me." Tears rolled from her eyes.

He knelt beside her. "Don't cry. Please. I made a terrible mistake asking you to marry me. I know you're a Christian woman, and I thought marriage would be the only way you'd agree to come with us."

Angry at her uncontrolled emotion, she grabbed a napkin from the holder and daubed her eyes. "You're an executive. You're strong and persuasive. Tell them you can't drag your kids that far away. They'll have to listen to you."

"And if they don't?" He rose and rested his hand on the back of her chair.

She lifted her eyes to his stress-filled face, trying to contain the ache in her heart. "They'll listen, Paul. They have to."

Chapter Two

Rose...I want you to marry me.

The words still echoed in Rose's ears two months later as she looked out the patio window of the lovely Victorian house that Paul had rented in Little Cloud. The setting was perfect for the twins—large yard, woods, creek, freedom. She watched them playing in the leaves, still amazed that in October trees had already turned colors.

Since arriving, she'd reviewed why she had finally agreed to come. But the answer was easy. The separation from the children had been dreadful. At night she would look at the moon and tell herself the same moon was hanging over Little Cloud, Minnesota, but the thought hadn't given her comfort as much as it had accentuated her isolation.

The children had become her life. After three weeks of Paul's pleading, she had agreed to relocate, and her fantasies had grown, with herself as mistress of a lovely home in Little Cloud—Paul coming home to dinner and telling her about his difficult day.

Then reality had set in. Things hadn't changed at all. As always, when Paul arrived home she returned to her quiet apartment. He had kept his promise—their deal, he called it. Not only was the apartment waiting when she arrived, but he'd bought her a new car.

Rose pulled her thoughts back to her task. She unloaded another carton of kitchen equipment and piled the empty box along with the others. She'd discovered the boxes in the back entry, waiting to be unpacked.

Time was fleeting, and Paul was late again. Even if he ate warmed-over meals, she had to feed the children.

Rose set the boxes aside while she checked the casserole in the oven, then called the children inside. They scampered through the doorway with leaves clinging to their clothes and dried grass on their shoes.

"Don't move," Rose said.

Colin stopped, then halted Kayla by the patio door.

"Look at your shoes," she said, heading for the broom. When she returned, Colin giggled.

"Shoes off and shake your jackets outside before you go upstairs…or I'll use this broom to shoo you back outside."

Colin dodged her teasing and even Kayla grinned as they slipped off their things and darted up the stairs.

Rose chuckled at her ploy. She used the broom as an idle threat. The twins would laugh when she grasped it and gave them a warning, but she'd learned they would usually do as she asked.

She swept up the debris and put away the broom. Then remembering Kayla's tangled hair, Rose headed for the staircase. "Kayla, please bring down your brush." If Kayla didn't respond, she prayed Colin would bring it.

In minutes, the children's footsteps reverberated on the stairs, and Colin arrived with Kayla's hairbrush.

"Thank you," Rose said, giving him a quick hug.

"Kayla, please come here."

Rose looked at the four-year-old and waited.

"Kayla, please."

The girl didn't move.

Rose's stomach twisted. Since their relocation the child had reverted to her old self before Rose had become their nanny. "Colin, please talk to your sister."

He repeated Rose's request, and without hesitation Kayla crossed the room and sat beside Rose.

She dragged the hairbrush across Kayla's long hair while the little girl sat statue-still. Rose wanted to take her in her arms and hug conversation out of her, but she'd tried that before and Kayla hadn't responded.

The day Rose had arrived in Little Cloud, Kayla had clung to her like moss to a tree trunk, but when it came to speaking, Rose never knew what to expect. She wondered if the child feared she'd leave again.

The thought broke Rose's heart. One day she would leave when Paul had no need for her anymore. A new panic jolted her. What did she have to go back to? She'd forsaken everything to make the move.

As Rose continued brushing Kayla's hair, static lifted the strands like magic fingers. "Look, Colin."

"She looks like a long-haired porcupine."

"I do not," Kayla said.

Rose heard curiosity in her voice. "Yes, you do. Colin's right." Praying it would work, Rose lifted the hand mirror in front of Kayla. "See for yourself."

Kayla giggled. "I do."

The child's words thrilled Rose. "But you're a very pretty porcupine."

Kayla looked at Rose—her smiling brown eyes so like her father's—and grinned.

Rose put down the hairbrush while an unexpected concern filled her mind. Kayla had begun preschool, and Rose prayed the other children weren't making fun of her and the teacher hadn't lost her patience. If so, Kayla could slide back even further. Maybe that's what was happening to her now.

The casserole's aroma filled the kitchen, and in moments the children and she were around the table, saying a blessing before they ate.

Time ticked past, and Rose finally sent the children to bed without seeing Paul. The scenario broke her heart.

The moon had risen high over the trees when Rose finally heard Paul's car pull into the drive. She stood and headed for the kitchen. He stepped through the doorway the same time she did.

"You look terrible," she said, witnessing the stress on his face and the tired look in his eyes.

He dropped his briefcase on a kitchen chair and gave a one-shoulder shrug. "I'm okay. The place is too laid-back for a well-run corporation. I'm trying to get the hang of their politics before implementing changes."

She moved to the refrigerator and brought out his dinner plate covered with plastic wrap. "How much longer will this go on?"

He shook his head and sank into a chair. "I don't know. It's taking more time than I planned, but I hope it ends soon."

"So do I." Rose slid the dish into the microwave and pressed the buttons.

"I'm sorry, Rose. I know this cuts into your time."

Her time? Rose's life revolved around this family. She had no life of her own. She wondered if he really understood. "It's not me I'm thinking of, Paul. It's the kids. They miss you."

"I know they do, and I miss them."

Rose looked at his expression and wished she'd kept quiet.

Chapter Three

Paul's head drooped, and Rose turned away, her heart aching for him. He wanted to be a good father, she knew.

When the buzzer sounded, she pulled a salad from the refrigerator and set the plate in front of him. "Would you like some coffee?"

"Sure," he said, "if you don't mind."

While she filled the coffeemaker, her mind whirred with memories. She recalled the day she'd arrived in Little Cloud. Paul had surprised her at the airport. She'd envisioned him dressed in a dark suit with a conservative tie and his hair immaculately combed as usual. Instead he'd worn jeans and a T-shirt beneath a plaid flannel jacket open at the front. His hair had seemed longer and shaggier. He'd looked as handsome and burly as a Minnesota lumberjack. She'd faltered before gaining control over her emotions. At that moment she had known she was in trouble.

"Rose."

Hearing the single word—her name—stirred her senses, and she swung around, sprinkling coffee grounds on the clean floor.

Paul noticed and smiled. "Sit with me while I eat."

She worked like a robot cleaning up the spill, then settled into a chair across from him.

Paul drew the napkin across his mouth. "How were the twins today?"

"Something good happened. Kayla spoke to me."

His face brightened. "What brought that on?"

She told him about Kayla's hair static. "I'm thinking I need to do something special with her. Colin spends his afternoons outside searching for all kinds of horrible bugs, while Kayla wants to play. I need to find ways to show her more attention."

"She'll eat that up."

"I hope so."

"How's she doing in school?" Paul asked.

"I haven't heard anything, but I plan to talk with the teacher next week and see if Kayla's communicating."

"Good. Thanks." Paul glanced at his empty plate. "I did a pretty good job."

"You did. You want that coffee now?"

His chair scraped on the tile as he pushed it back. "Sure. Then we can sit in the living room and talk."

Her pulse jumped at his words. "Talk?"

Paul gave a tired grin. "Just talk. I need a friend."

He needed a friend. So did she, but any relationship beyond the boss-employee boundary sent chills down her back.

"You go ahead," she said, "and I'll bring it in."

Paul vanished through the doorway, and Rose stared at the empty space. She poured the coffee and carried it into the living room. Paul had lit a fire, and the warmth beckoned her. She handed him a cup, then settled nearby.

Silence surrounded them, except for the snap of the embers sending up a sprinkle of red and yellow sparks. She watched the glow, waiting for Paul to talk. The longer she waited the more uncomfortable she felt.

This wasn't the first time Paul had asked her to visit before she made the lonely ten-mile trek home. Sometimes she wondered if she'd made a mistake letting him persuade her to relocate. But she couldn't blame him solely. Her heart had made her decision.

"Why so quiet?" Rose asked, wishing he'd say something.

"Thinking about the kids. I know I'm letting them down when they need me."

"You are. I'm not going to soften it. They wait all afternoon for you to come home, then go to bed missing you." She missed him, too, if she were honest.

"I'll do better soon. Promise."

"Promise?" She'd heard that before. She knew he had good intentions, but—

"Please trust me. I'm trying to get things settled."

Trust me. She'd heard that before, too.

They fell into silence again, and Rose relived the hurt and humiliation of nearly two years earlier when she had learned that her fiancé—her boss—was cheating on her. While she was chattering about her marriage plans and spitting out her hopes and dreams, the whole office staff knew about…

The memory caught in her throat. She'd stopped shedding tears. Now she'd hardened herself. That day, she had returned Don's ring and walked away from her plush job. Never again. She'd trusted a man once. She had garnered too much experience, too much doubt and too much humiliation to make that mistake again.

"Sometimes I feel strange, sitting here with you."

"Strange? Why?" He looked at her for the first time since she'd brought him his coffee.

"Many times you've asked me to sit after you get home late and we chat like old friends…and yet I'm your employee."

"Rose, please," he said, grasping the arm of the chair and leaning closer. "You're more like a friend, not an employee. I have employees at the plant."

Friends. Employer. Employee. She gazed at Paul's profile. He was good-looking and stable. She wanted to trust him. His light brown hair shimmered with highlights in the glow from the fire. But she'd let good looks sway her once. Not again.

Rose paused a minute, drawn by the gold and red leaves fluttering to the patio. The children's laughter drifted in from outside. They seemed to love the outdoors and had spent time after school playing hide-and-seek, then switching to tag as they tripped and tumbled onto the broad expanse of lawn. When they bounded from the ground, the leaves attached to their clothing like colorful patchwork.

Looking out, Rose smiled until she recalled Colin offering to show her a snake he'd found. She wanted no part of any creature that didn't walk on four legs or two. That included bugs and spiders.

Rose looked at the clock, knowing she should be doing other things, but none of the options struck her fancy. The fresh air had a greater pull.

She climbed the stairs, grabbed a sweatshirt and tugged it over her blouse. Back in the kitchen, she stepped through the doorway to the covered patio. A pleasant breeze carried the scent of damp earth and dried foliage to her.

A leaf rake leaned against the house as if calling to her, and she grasped it while the children beckoned her to join the fun. While the twins grabbed handfuls of the dried leaves and tossed them her way, she raked them into a pile. Because of the noise the children were making, Rose didn't hear Paul arrive until she felt him shove a handful of leaves down her neck.

"This is war," she called, gathering her own crispy weapons and charging toward him.

Still dressed in his suit, he captured her hand and held it fast while his other one grasped her waist as if fending her off. She tried to wiggle free, but he kept them close.

When their eyes met, something passed between them. Awareness? Concern? Surprise? Before she could decide, he pulled away with a laugh. "Unfair," he said, dashing across the lawn. "Let me go change."

In a flash he was gone, and the children joined her using their hands while she piled the leaves into a high mound.

When Paul returned, dressed in jeans and a pullover, he brought along another leaf rake and a camera. They took a break to snap photos of the twins, then Paul and Rose with the autumn colors as their background.

Finally they returned to work. But before Rose realized what Paul was plotting, he grabbed her rake and tossed her into the colorful heap. Leaves billowed around her, catching in her hair. They crackled as she shifted to rise, ready to make her own attack, but the children had already begun the job.

With the twins against Paul's back, he tumbled forward and landed beside her with a thwack. The crisp pile crunched beneath Rose's elbow as she tried to move out of the way, but Paul turned his face so close the nearness unsettled her. Before she could escape, the children joined the battle with armfuls of gold and orange.

Playful, Paul became her protector, blocking the children's attack. As he shifted, their noses brushed in the chaos, making her heart flutter like a lone leaf clinging to an overhead bough.

The twins jumped into the fray, and they became a tangle of arms and legs until she and Paul sorted them out. They clamored from the strewn mound, their cheerful voices ringing in her ears.

For once Rose knew why she'd come to Little Cloud.

This was home.

Paul stepped back and feasted on the sight of their leaf-strewn clothing. The children's smiles had never been brighter. His gaze shifted to Rose, her cheeks ruddy, her eyes glistening with their fun. His chest tightened.

He'd managed to convince her to come to Little Cloud. He'd called it a deal. Agreement. Contract. Whatever. He had dragged Rose to Minnesota to make life easier for him. He'd given little thought to her needs, and now he'd asked her to be his friend. An unpleasant sensation rattled through him. Had he turned Rose's life upside down only to offer her a business deal?

He studied Rose's slender frame. He loved her broad smile when the children made her laugh with their antics. He couldn't help but wonder why she'd never married and what had caused her to leave a good paying job and end up baby-sitting for his kids. She'd never told him, and he felt it too personal to ask.

But then, who was he to question anyone? Since Della's death, he'd had to learn to live without a woman. But time had passed, and he felt his mind and heart wakening to a need. His gaze shifted to the children. They deserved a mother.

He grabbed the rake and dragged the thought away along with the leaves. "Let's get this back into a pile, and we can have a bonfire." He had to do something to stop the ache that had grown inside him.

Rose excused herself and headed for the house while Paul tugged at the leaves, drawing in the scent of autumn and a hint of winter's cold. When he'd made a high mound, he lit the leaves and watched the flame grow, crackling and spiraling smoke into the air.

Despite his attempt to forget, his concern for Rose returned again. The children were a handful, yet the dearest kids on earth. But they were nonstop, and so was Rose's life. He had to give Rose a break. She put up with too many long, stressful days.

He thought of his aunt Inez, who'd been so helpful when he first arrived. He'd been blessed to have her so near. Asking her to help again seemed pushing his luck, but he had to do something until his work life calmed down. He would think of something special for Rose.

Chapter Four

Rose walked across the lawn, watching the sparks sail into the sky like fairy dust. "Pretty," she said. As she stood beside Paul, a shiver coursed through her.

"Cold?"

"A little," she said, stepping closer to the fire. She eyed the trees not far away. "When the woods start on fire, remember I warned you."

He laughed and slid his arm around her back, giving her an amiable squeeze. As he let go, Colin bounded toward them with Kayla on his heels.

Paul tousled their heads. "What did you learn today in school?"

"We learned about the Ojibways," Colin said.

Kayla jigged in front of him. "We're going on a trip to the field."

"To the field?" He looked at Rose with a puzzled expression.

"It's a field trip," she said. "They're going to the Mille Lacs Museum next week. I put the permission form on the kitchen counter."

"A field trip. That sounds fun." He paused, then spoke what seemed an afterthought. "Do you like the teacher? I don't think I've asked." He glanced at Rose.

"No, you haven't," Rose said. She saw him flinch from her biting comment. Usually she felt bad about what she said, but not today. Paul had to face responsibility.

"She's nice," Kayla said as she spun away.

Rose watched the children run off to search for more leaves and tried to forget her comment. The children danced around the flames like the Ojibways they'd learned about in school. Rose drew in the acrid scent of burning leaves permeating her hair and clothes. But she didn't care. She loved the glow of the flames and the feeling of being one with nature and the joy of watching the twins.

"You're quiet," Paul said, closing the distance between them.

"Just thinking how peaceful it is." She brushed a leaf from her hair.

Paul set the rake in front of him and leaned against it while she studied his face. He stared at the curling flames in silence, and Rose wondered what was on his mind.

Finally he shifted. "I've not only neglected the kids, Rose, but I've worked you overtime. I can't thank you enough for your dedication."

"That's what I'm here for." Her response punctuated her situation. She had no life of her own. No friends. No co-workers. No reason for a day off. She'd made some progress at the church, but no friendships yet.

Paul rested his hand on her shoulder and gave it a gentle squeeze. "Still, I owe you some time off. I'll check with Aunt Inez and see if she could take over for an afternoon or two."

"And take her away from her social clubs or church ladies? You can't do that."

Paul chuckled. "I'm sure she'd give up an afternoon. She should be happy to have us so close."

Rose's curiosity was piqued. "I've always wondered how it happens that your aunt lives in Little Cloud."

"It's not really a coincidence. Uncle Lucas was a big honcho with the company. In fact, he helped me get my job with them after I graduated from college. Right after he was transferred here. Aunt Inez hated it."

"She doesn't hate it now."

"No, it's been her home for many years, and she loves the place now."

Rose could understand his aunt's qualms. Even thinking about the cold weather that she could already feel heading their way set her on edge.

Paul shifted toward the bonfire and caught some straying leaves. "My uncle was well respected, and the company flourished, but after he died, things changed. New leadership. New ideas. I don't know."

"So that's why they sent you here. Bring back a Stewart and the company will come to life again."

"Something like that." He reached over and brushed his hand against her cheek. "You have a decoration," he said, reaching up to pull a leaf from her hair. He brushed it against her cheek before tossing it onto the fire.

At that moment Rose enjoyed their closeness, a kind of simple sharing that seemed so warm and intimate. She raised her eyes beyond the drifting sparks to a small twinkling diamond in the heavens and prayed life could feel this good forever.

Rose rested her palm against Kayla's shoulder as she waited to speak with the teacher at the Bright Beginnings

Children's Center. Colin hovered nearby, too, and Rose knew he was anxious to have her meet their teacher.

As the other parent stepped away, Miss Gladwin turned toward her with a smile. "Well, now, it's your turn, Mrs. Stewart, eh?"

Rose opened her mouth, but before she could correct the woman, Colin spoke up. "Her name is Mrs. Danby."

"Miss Danby," Rose said. "Mrs. Stewart is deceased."

"Oh." The woman's face took on a puzzled look, and she glanced back at the papers. "Then you are…?"

"The nanny. I care for the children while their father works."

"Nanny?" She gave Rose a curious look. "My word, I thought you were the twins' mother."

Rose waited a moment for her to continue.

She didn't.

"I need to talk with you about Kayla," Rose said, hoping to help her recollect their previous conversation.

"What is this about, eh?" She looked at the children, then back at Rose.

Rose drew up her shoulders and eyed the twins, wishing they'd wander off and give Rose time to talk privately. "She's shy."

"Yes, your son…I mean, Colin mentioned that."

"Kayla's father would like to know how she's doing," Rose said, being more direct.

"Why can't Mr. Stewart come to see me instead of—"

"The nanny?" Rose felt her hand tremble. "Mr. Stewart works long hours. He's planning to meet you when he can find the time." She had said more than she wanted. "I just need an answer. Is Kayla communicating with you or not?"

Miss Gladwin turned her attention toward Kayla. "Why, we get along just fine, eh?"

Kayla gave her a nod and looked at Rose with questioning eyes.

Rose felt her defenses rise. She grasped Kayla's hand and drew her closer. "If you have any problems, please call the Stewart home. We'd be happy to do whatever you suggest."

Miss Gladwin gave her a distracted smile while Rose grasped the children's hands and tugged them out to the parking lot. She unlocked the minivan door, then gulped the brisk air while the children scrambled into the back and clamped their seat belts.

Collecting her thoughts, she got into the van and pulled away. Paul had said the town was different, and it was. Much of it was wonderful. She enjoyed the slower pace, but she wished she hadn't been made to feel that she was nobody.

Paul had given her the apartment and the car. She should be grateful. Instead she felt depressed when she had to leave the cozy Victorian for her empty place. She thought of her friends back in California. She missed them. She missed the warm weather and sunshine, but when she was there she missed the twins. And she missed Paul.

She had no answer and saw no happy ending in sight.

At home the children headed outside to tug the rakes around the yard in hopes of another bonfire. The sun that had seemed warm when she entered the children's center earlier had slipped behind a cloud, and a gray haze settled over the sky and her mood. She watched the children while her mind took her to places she didn't want to go.

The day had dragged. Rose's mind dwelled on her vacillating mind-set. One minute she loved being in Little

Cloud, the next she longed to go back to L.A. Her unrest had grown during her visit with Miss Gladwin, who had looked at her like some kind of usurper.

Sometime after dinner, Rose saw Kayla yawn, and looked at her watch. Bedtime again. Her heart ached for the children. She stood and wrapped her arm around Kayla.

"Time for bed," she said, knowing she'd hear groans.

"I want to wait up for Daddy," Colin whined.

Rose used her free hand to tousle his hair.

Kayla's sad eyes caught Rose's. "Me, too."

Each time Kayla spoke to her, Rose's chest swelled with joy. Each day Kayla had expanded her world to include Rose, and hopefully she would also include her preschool teacher.

Rose lifted an eyebrow. "I could sweep you both upstairs with the broom."

They ducked from her grasp with giggles.

"But here's what we'll do," Rose said. "Get ready for bed, then I'll come up and tuck you in."

Colin's eyes narrowed. "But we want—"

"You can keep your light on, and if you hear your dad come home before you're sleeping, you can come down to say good-night. Is that a deal?" As the word left her mouth, she cringed. Her whole life had become a deal.

The children agreed with the second plan and scampered up the stairs. She listened to the sounds above her, feeling a brief sense of completeness before it was barraged by her perplexing unhappiness.

In minutes, Rose heard the side door open, and she headed for the kitchen. When she came through the doorway, Paul stood in the middle of the room, his eyes looking tired.

His caring face triggered Rose's emotions and the tension

of the day rushed in like a flood. The dam she'd built for the children crumbled, and the tears poured from her. She lowered her head, hoping he wouldn't see.

"What's wrong?" he said, dropping his briefcase on the floor and rushing to her side. "Is it the kids?"

She could only shake her head, feeling out of control and disgusted with her lack of restraint.

Paul slid his arm around her and pressed her head to his suit coat. She leaned against his firm body, holding her arms against her chest, but longing to wrap them around his protective frame. When she'd calmed enough to talk, she pulled her head away from his dampened suit jacket. "I'm sorry. When I saw you, I fell apart."

His frightened expression tugged her back to reason. "The kids are fine. I sent them upstairs for bed." She wiped her eyes with the back of her hand. "It's me."

He shook his head as if trying to make sense of her words. "What's wrong?"

"I don't know. I'm depressed."

"Daddy!" Kayla bounded into the room, followed by Colin. Both had dressed in their pajamas, and Rose could smell the minty scent of toothpaste.

As disheartened as she felt, Rose was pleased they'd done as she asked and even brushed their teeth.

Paul gave them a hug. "Daddy wants to change clothes, so come upstairs and I'll tuck you in." He beckoned to them, then signaled Rose. "We'll talk later."

She nodded, understanding what it was like to be a parent. Much of what seemed important was held for later, away from little ears.

Chapter Five

While Paul put the children to bed, Rose warmed his dinner, pondering what she should do and why she should do anything at all. The microwave buzzer sounded as Paul returned to the kitchen.

"Hungry?" she asked.

"I'm sorry I was so late tonight," he said. "It's been a difficult day."

"I know. You eat, and I'll start a fire."

Rose left him alone and went to the living room, knowing now wasn't the time to talk. She lit the fire in the grate, but the icy tendrils that crept through her heart couldn't be warmed by heat. She had to leave the cozy house and head across town to her own home—rooms that didn't seem like home at all.

Settling in front of the hearth, Rose leaned back and listened to the quiet. Soon Paul's steps sounded in the hallway, and he appeared carrying two mugs.

"Coffee," he said. "Yours has cream. That's how you like it, right?"

She nodded, pleased that he remembered. Rose accepted the cup and took a sip. The drink rolled across her tongue and spread an inner warmth in her chest. In silence she studied Paul's face.

He didn't ask questions. He ran his finger around the mug's rim, waiting. The silence lingered, and though she wanted to talk, Rose felt empty of words.

"I don't like seeing you this way, Rose," Paul said. "You've always been so upbeat. Tell me what's wrong?"

Rose drank in his kindness, but what could she say? She didn't know what was wrong.

Paul sipped his coffee without prodding.

"I should be happy, but I'm…miserable."

"Rose, I'm—I…" His words faded while he looked at her with so much concern it broke her heart.

"It's nothing you can do," she said. "I suppose I'm homesick. You know, the little girl goes to camp for the first time and misses her family." The image weighed heavily on her. "Except that's what's wrong. All my relatives live on the East Coast. You are my family. That struck me today. If I did go back to California, I'd be going back to nothing. Sure, I have friends that I miss, but—"

He lowered his eyes. "No apartment. No job. No—"

"No future."

He opened his mouth to speak, then closed it as if he couldn't rebut what she'd said.

Rose hadn't intended him to feel guilty. "I talked with the teacher today."

"How did it go? Is Kayla having problems?"

She shook her head. It wasn't Kayla. Rose was having problems with herself, but how could she explain that? "I think she's okay. She understands Kayla's shy."

Paul's face darkened. "Something's upset you."

"It was silly. Nothing important."

"It upset you, Rose, so it *is* important."

She gave in and told him about the teacher's reaction to her visit. "I felt useless—like I was a woman playing mother to the kids. She didn't want me there."

He closed the distance between them and knelt in front of her. "Rose, these people aren't questioning you. You're a novelty. A new face in town. A nanny. They've probably never heard the term except on TV. That part is probably more interesting to them than anything else."

Rose bit her lip. "Maybe, but sometimes I think I should go back."

"Go back? You mean to L.A?" He rose and sat beside her. "Please don't think about that. I won't let you."

She felt her back stiffen. "This is a job, Paul. I can leave anytime. I have to do what's best for me." Though she'd made the statement, the children came into her thoughts. What was best for them?

"I suppose it is a job," he said, looking as if he'd been slapped.

A job to her? Yes and no. The question was, what was it to him? "I didn't mean it like that. I just—" Just what? She just wanted to be a wife and mother. She wanted... what? She looked at his handsome, worried face and knew what she wanted.

Like a movie, her life played out in her mind's eye—past and present. But what about the future? She'd never been more content in her life than she had with Paul and the twins. She loved the kids. Life didn't seem worthwhile without them. And Paul? She knew the answer. She was falling in love with him. But as hopeless as it was, her mind kept asking—what if?

Paul looked at Rose and waited, one hand on her arm, the other flexing with tension. What did he expect of her? She'd given up everything to follow him, and why? What did he have to offer her? The answer: nothing.

Maybe he should encourage her to leave. If he did, he might be motivated to find a woman—a wife, someone to take care of the house and love his children. His contemplation frightened him. He sounded cold and unloving. He didn't want a relationship like that. But what did he want?

"I've only been thinking about me," she said, "and not what's important. I need to give my problems to God."

His heart sank at the sadness in her voice. "You've focused on us." What was he doing to her? Condemning her to a life of emptiness to keep her with him as a housekeeper and nanny. Using her to make life easier for himself. Rose was a beautiful woman—charming, witty, confident.

He wanted to tell her how wonderful she was, but she wouldn't believe him. He'd already frightened her once with his hasty proposal. Why had he been so stupid?

"You need to spend time on yourself, Rose. I know I work long hours and keep you here longer than—"

He stopped in the middle of the sentence and reeled with the awareness. Though his mind was plagued with company issues throughout the day, his deeper focus had left him longing to come home to this house and the twins. He'd set his mind on doing something for Rose, but what had happened?

She deserved to be pampered. He vowed to do what he could to bring a smile to Rose's face, to make her eyes light up and to make her move to Little Cloud worthwhile.

"It's okay," she said. "I feel better now."

He tilted her chin upward and looked into her eyes. "I want you to feel the best, Rose, not just better." Paul let his gaze linger on her mouth, compelled by an unexpected urge. Confused, he redirected his thoughts. Apparently he'd been without a woman too long.

Paul closed his eyes, wondering what had gotten into him. He'd never survive this deal he'd made unless he stopped looking at Rose as a woman.

"It's Daddy!" Kayla called.

The children darted from the living room while Rose held a print of an oil painting, trying to decide where it would look best. If she were honest, she'd admit she didn't like the painting, but this wasn't her house.

Paul came through the doorway with the twins tagging beside him, both talking at once. "Let me catch my breath." He plopped into the recliner, and his eyes widened. "What's happened in here?"

"Unpacking boxes," she said. "I thought it was time this room looked like a home."

"Looks good." His gaze traveled the room, then focused on the kids.

The pleasure in his face warmed Rose, and she sat on the edge of the sofa. Still holding the painting, she let the children tell their stories.

"What's up? Have you been helping Rose?"

Kayla's head bounced like a rubber ball. "We picked out border and paint."

Paul gave Rose another questioning look. "Border and paint?"

"For their rooms," Rose said. "I'm going to paint during the week, and maybe on the weekend we can get the border up."

"Border and paint," he repeated. "Sounds like an exciting weekend." He gave her a teasing wink.

"We'll show it to you," Kayla said. The twins scampered from the room, leaving a moment of silence.

"I unpacked the boxes that were in the dining room. The

photographs of the kids and…your wife are on the built-in shelves. I hope that's what you wanted."

Paul rose and ambled across the room, his gaze scanning the work that she'd done. "It looks good, Rose." He lifted the photograph of Della and looked at it a moment, then turned to her. "I think I'll give this to Kayla, and I have one in my room for Colin." He laid the framed photo face-down. "I think it's time—"

"Changes are good in a new house," Rose said, hoping to ease the tension. She lifted the painting. "I hung some of the artwork, but I wasn't sure about this one."

He shook his head. "I never liked that piece. Della wanted it. Let's just put it away. I hear there's an autumn art and craft show in a couple of weeks. Maybe we could find something new for that wall."

"I'd be happy to look," she said. Change was difficult, but it could be positive. It could turn life from status quo to innovative. She'd had a big taste of that lately.

Paul moved closer, his hands in his pockets. "I'm trying to get my time regulated at work. I don't want to spend every weekend glued to my office chair, and I don't want to disappoint the kids. Count on me for the weekend."

Rose opened her mouth, but her words were drowned by the kids' chatter as they ran into the room dragging the borders, which trailed dangerously under their feet. She watched the exuberance of the twins as they described plans for their bedrooms. Paul slowed them to a walk, and Rose sank into the sofa, her heart full.

Paul stood in Colin's bedroom, reading the instructions on hanging the border. It seemed simple enough. He felt guilty having dumped the painting job totally on Rose. She'd done a good job. He gazed at the soft-blue room that coordinated with the race-car border Colin had chosen. Kayla's room was as pink as her cheeks. She'd picked a design of pink hearts with a smattering of pastel flowers. Rose had guided them well.

The door banged below—Rose had come home from church. His pulse gave a jolt. Too much coffee, he speculated. He set the border on Colin's bed and descended the stairs. The children had already met her in the kitchen, and he could hear them whining about lunch. Paul winced. He could have at least taken care of that. He'd become too job focused. The promise he'd made to pamper Rose had slid from his thoughts.

When he came through the doorway he expected a sharp look from Rose for messing up yesterday by working another Saturday. Instead, she smiled.

"How was church?" he asked.

"Nice."

He wanted to ask more, but her attention turned to other things. She slipped off her jacket, laid her handbag on the counter and began making lunch.

"I'm getting everything ready to put up the borders. Okay?" he asked.

A look of surprise brightened her face. "Sure, if you don't mind helping."

He wanted to hug her. "I should have helped you with the painting. I'll make up for it today."

He hurried away, gathering ladders and water containers to use for dipping the prepasted paper. When he had everything assembled, Rose came up the stairs with a sandwich on a paper plate. She'd thought of him again.

"Thanks. I should have made lunch for the kids."

"It's okay," she said. "Let me change, and then we can decide who does what."

It wasn't okay at all, but he turned his attention to the task and reread the instructions.

Rose returned wearing jeans and a pullover. She stood inside the doorway and leaned against the doorjamb. Though twenty-seven, she looked like a teenager with her slender figure and her hair in a gentle curve at her jawline. The sun's rays shining through the window touched her tawny locks with golden highlights. She seemed as fresh and dewy as her name. He felt old at thirty-one.

"Ready?" he asked. As the question left him, two sets of feet thumped in the hallway, and the twins came into the room.

"Can we help?" Colin asked.

Paul looked at Rose for the answer.

"Good idea," she said. "How about the men hang their border in this room while Kayla and I take care of hers."

"Like a contest?" Kayla asked.

Rose gave Kayla a one-arm hug. "Why not? Last one finished cooks dinner."

"Okay," Paul said, wanting to squelch the idea. Still, he was taller. Hanging border would be a snap.

As Kayla and Rose darted from the room, Paul looked at the wall and drew in a breath. If Rose could do it, he could. "Okay, Colin. Let's get to work."

He looked at his young son and wondered how the two of them were going to hang the border way up there.

Rose closed the bedroom door, anticipating their task. Border at the top of the wall seemed impossible.

"What can I do?" Kayla asked, her cheeks rosy and her eyes wide.

You can give me a huge hug, Rose thought, gazing at

the sweet child. In the past days, Kayla had forgotten not to talk. She'd opened like a blossom in spring.

An idea struck Rose. "Here's my idea. Let's put the border here." She held the border at the same height as the chair railing. Kayla would enjoy it at eye level.

"Okay, and I can see it lower," Kayla said.

They became a team. Rose used a yardstick to mark the height, and when she finished, Kayla dipped the border into the water and held an end while Rose smoothed it along the wall. In an hour the job was done, and they crossed the hallway. When Rose pushed open the door, she laughed.

Paul stood on the ladder with border draped over his shoulder. His jeans and shirt were soaked and glue clung to his cheek. He'd finished only one side of the room.

"We're finished," she said from the doorway.

He spun around gaping. "Finished?"

Kayla clapped her hands and crunched down with her giggles. "You look silly, Daddy."

He climbed down the ladder with an expression of disbelief. He pulled the border from his neck and grasped her shoulders with both hands, moving her ahead of him.

When they entered the room, he stopped cold. "You cheated. I thought it had to be on top."

"I didn't tell you where it had to go." She reached up and brushed the gob of paste from his cheek while the children clustered at his sides. "Paste," Rose said, holding up her finger to show him the evidence.

"Looks good. You two did a good job, but if you want to eat dinner tonight, I need some help," he said.

She acquiesced, happy to spend the time with him working on the project.

The twins became bored and wandered away. Rose climbed the ladder while Paul used the one from Kayla's bedroom. Their conversation rolled like that of old friends as they smoothed and dipped, adding each long stretch of border until the end was in sight. One final swipe of the cloth to smooth the last piece, and Rose descended the ladder.

"Looks really good," Paul said, wrapping his arm around her shoulders. "We make a great team." He shifted his gaze to her face. "Do you like it?"

Like it? She loved feeling his arm around her. "I do." Her double meaning skittered through the air.

Paul gave her a gentle squeeze and glanced at his watch. "It's late. How about fast food?"

"What about my home-cooked meal?"

He pressed the tip of her nose. "Tomorrow night?"

"Right." She grinned, knowing he'd wheedle out of their deal.

Chapter Six

Rose sat at the kitchen window, watching the children play in the backyard. That morning when she'd taken them to preschool, frost had clung to a few green plants trying to brave the nippy winds. By the time the sun had risen to its zenith, the foliage lay limp against the ground.

She decided to brave her battle. She'd found comfort and strength at her new church. The Sunday before, she'd left the church feeling guilty as the Scripture reading rang in her head. "O you of little faith... Do not worry about tomorrow, for tomorrow will worry about itself. Each day has enough trouble of its own. Do not judge, or you, too, will be judged."

She had worried, and she had judged Paul. He'd made promises that he'd meant to keep but often didn't. He'd asked her to trust him, but trust had been difficult since Don's betrayal.

Yet when she arrived home from worship, God had answered her prayer. Paul was ready to help with the border. They'd had fun, and she sensed a change in their relationship.

In the past weeks, church attendance had drawn her

closer to God. She realized moping wasn't going to get her anywhere. Until the Lord directed her otherwise, she would continue to be a nanny for the twins, and if Paul came home with a woman, she would have to…

That thought unsettled her. There was one issue she hadn't resolved—her feelings for Paul. He hadn't helped the situation either, because the past week he'd arrived home earlier than expected and even surprised her once by cooking dinner. One evening they had listened to the children relive their trip to the museum. Another night he'd taken them to a family movie. She'd become a part of their lives, but sadly, Rose knew one day it would end.

Through the window Rose saw the children bounding toward the house, then caught sight of Paul. He crouched and clasped the children in his arms. She longed to be there, too, wrapped in his strength and comfort.

She pushed the useless thought aside and looked toward the sky, noticing the sun had sunk below the treetops. Night came fast in late autumn, and the wooded setting only added to her feeling of solitude.

Paul headed toward the house, and Rose moved from the window. "Hi," she said as he entered. "You're home early,"

"Sure am."

She recognized his conspiring look. "What's up?"

"Aunt Inez agreed to sit with the kids tonight."

Her heart skipped. "Why?"

"You need a night out. We're celebrating."

"Celebrating?"

"I've finally made progress at the plant. I know what's causing the problems, and today I put together a plan to implement the changes." He shrugged. "I realize it'll still take time."

"And that's what you're celebrating?"

He moved closer. "No, but here's my good news. L.A. is sending someone to give me a hand for a few weeks."

"That should be a relief."

"It is. I'm anxious to spend more time with the kids." He reached out and touched her arm. "But we'll still want you to hang around. The place is too quiet without you."

"You'd get used to it quick enough," she said, wondering if he would miss her. "Where are we going?"

"First to the arts and crafts fair. Do you realize that Christmas will be here before we know it? November's here in four days. Then Thanksgiving. Then Christmas."

Christmas. The word washed over her. "You mean we're going Christmas shopping?"

"If you remember, I suggested a while back we look for a new painting to go behind the sofa."

That seemed ages ago, and she'd forgotten. "Okay, but you said 'first.' What's second?"

"That's a surprise."

Walking beside Rose, Paul enjoyed the closeness. She was a lovely woman. Her smile, her thoughtfulness, her joy—she exhibited so many attributes he admired.

He adjusted the package clutched in his arms. Since they'd entered the Elks Lodge, Rose had already goaded him into buying Christmas decorations, a huge wreath and numerous gifts for the children.

At the end of the aisle Paul spotted a booth selling artwork. He moved closer, drawn by a large watercolor that captured his interest—a wooded setting, a stream and two leaves, stems still locked together, floating along on the ripples. Elusive lines, muted colors, yet a vibrant image. He thought of himself as a leaf floating along life's river, caught on the ripples with no turning back. Yet he drifted alone. The picture filled him with hope. Two leaves glided side by side, their stems bent upward toward the sun filtering through the trees. Hope and completeness, two leaves as one.

"It's beautiful," Rose said.

He turned toward her and realized she was gazing at the same painting.

"It touches me here," she said, resting her palm against her heart. "I see togetherness through the rough spots, a kind of solidarity. I can't explain it."

Neither could he. "I'm going to buy it. It'll look good over the sofa."

"It's perfect." Her smile warmed him.

Paul was amazed at their oneness. So often they thought the same. Yet other times he sensed her wariness—her sensitivity—and he wished he understood.

He paid for the watercolor, then moved on. Within moments Rose stopped at another booth.

"I like candles in the windows at Christmas," she said, surveying the decorative tapers.

Candles in the windows. Rose's exuberance fueled that Christmas feeling that made Paul want to burst into a chorus of "Joy to the World."

Before they moved farther, she turned to him. "Thinking of Christmas, I'd like to take the children to Sunday school, if you wouldn't mind. I think they should have the chance to know what Jesus' birthday really means."

Paul caught his breath—another way he'd neglected his children. "Sure. It'll be good for them."

Rose gave him a pleased look, then moved on ahead.

He'd never been given a strong faith upbringing, but Della had thought it was important, and before she died they'd all been going to church. Paul recalled it had become a comfort. It gave him something to cling to when times got rough. But when Della died, his faith did, too. He agreed. The twins needed a chance to learn about Jesus on their own.

Something to cling to. The words surged through his mind. He'd needed something to cling to these past months. He'd hung on to his problems as if they were treasures. They'd caused him to become even more self-focused, and he hadn't given God a chance to direct him. Had the stress in his life been a reflection of his weak faith? If this was the Lord's way to give him a swift kick, He'd done a good job.

Another booth caught Rose's interest. She shuffled through a display of handcrafted wooden puzzles. "Look. The kids'll love these. I'll buy a couple for Christmas."

He agreed. They were intriguing.

She selected two for each child, and he wanted to hug her for being so generous.

Paul toted the growing mound of packages, and when they arrived where they'd begun, he stopped her. "Are we about finished? Remember, we have one more place to go."

She tilted her head with questioning eyes. "I know." She gave him a wry grin. "I won't ask."

He gave her a wink, but before he moved, he had to ask one last question. "Out of all these gifts, didn't you find one thing you liked for yourself?"

She thought a minute. "I loved those bracelets. The ones with the fused glass beads. They were beautiful, but too expensive for my taste."

"I remember," he said while his gaze darted in the direction he thought he'd seen the booth. "Do you mind waiting a minute while I find a rest room?"

"Not at all," she said. She reached for the packages, and he handed her a few and then set the others against the exit wall. "I'll be right back."

He had no idea where he was going, but he hoped to find a back entrance into the craft show. As he rounded a corner, he spotted a doorway and maneuvered his way down the crowded aisles to the booth selling stained glass.

In only a minute he found the perfect bracelet, with translucent glass beads in pastel blue and amber, each bead connected with small gold links. It was lovely and fragile like Rose. He paid the money, dropped the package into his pocket and wended his way to the exit.

"Ready?" he asked.

"Can't wait," she said, her voice dubious. Rose returned his packages, and she carried the watercolor.

The night was chilly, and the scent of snow filled the air. They hurried to the car. On their way, he and Rose talked about everyday things, and when Paul reached the town, he followed the signs to Historic Log Village.

"Where are we?" Rose asked.

"Crosslake. It's north of Little Cloud." He spotted another marker and turned. "I think you'll enjoy this. You deserve a little fun."

When the parking lot came into view, Paul pulled into an available slot and opened the door for her. Her smile was illumined by moonlight, and it roused his exhilarated feelings. He paid the admission, and they were each handed a lit candle. Rose sent him a curious look, but once inside the Historic Log Village, the purpose was clear.

Rose grasped his arm and released a breathless sigh. "It's beautiful."

He agreed. In front of them lights flickered in the darkness as visitors were taken back in time to the days of the pioneer settlers. Candles brightened a turn-of-the-century schoolhouse, a restored logger's shack and bunkhouse. Workers were dressed in costumes of the day and offered them cups of cider as they made their way along, learning about the days of the Minnesota pioneers.

"The twins would love this," Rose said, her eyes glinting brighter than the candles. "You'll have to bring them here. They would learn so much."

"We will," Paul said, wanting Rose to share the pleasure.

She paused to sip the cider, and Paul was mesmerized by the shape of her mouth and the soft look of her well-formed lips. To quell his thoughts, Paul swigged down the tart juice.

He disposed of their empty cups, amazed at the realization that had washed over him. For so long, he'd wanted a mother for the children, and lately he'd felt an urge for a companion. Tonight he found one standing beside him. He'd never appreciated Rose's charm and beauty until now.

She turned to face him, the candle flickering a soft light over her lovely face. "Thank you for the surprise."

"You're welcome." Unbidden, he drew her into an embrace. "You deserve much more," he whispered into her hair. She felt fragile against his chest, and a gentle fragrance of fruits and spices surrounded her. Puzzled by his feelings, he released her.

Bewilderment covered her face, probably matching his own confusion. He lifted his gaze to the sky. *Lord, tell me what You want. I need Your direction.*

Chapter Seven

Rose sat in her too-quiet apartment. In the dim lamplight the moon spread its glow along the living-room rug like silver fingers.

Sleep had escaped her. The evening had been wonderful. The twinkling candles, like fireflies, had danced along in the darkness. The historic buildings, the costumed workers, the tangy cider had made the evening more than memorable. Most of all, Paul had embraced her.

He'd changed so much. In past weeks he'd been arriving home earlier than expected. The children were ecstatic. They had time to enjoy his company before bedtime. Watching them lifted Rose's spirits.

But it was more than that. He'd mellowed. Paul seemed more sensitive, almost as if he were pampering her. She loved it. Yet she distrusted it. They were from two different worlds. He had an education, a position and polish. She'd become employed following one year of business school. She'd never traveled. She'd experienced little. She had so little to offer a man like Paul.

Often Paul looked at her curiously as if he didn't understand why she reacted as she did. She'd never been open with him about her broken engagement and the issues it had caused. The situation had destroyed her trust and confidence. She'd been pitied, and no one wanted pity.

Had Paul pitied her, too? Was he pampering her to motivate her to stay in Little Cloud? She couldn't ask him. She would have to explain too much.

Rose shifted in the chair and reached for her Bible. She scanned the pages until her eyes focused on Proverbs 3:5, 6. "Trust in the Lord with all your heart and lean not on your own understanding. In all your ways acknowledge Him, and He will make your paths straight."

That's what she needed, a straight path. Rose had tried hard to let God lead her, but she fought Him every step. *Lean not on your own understanding.* She would make that her motto.

Rose placed the Bible back on the table and switched off the lamp. The moon guided her steps, but before returning to bed she pulled back the curtain. Tonight she saw a melon-colored moon. The mountains and valleys that created the moon's face were clear, and the moon seemed nearer than its great distance from earth.

Melon moon. Melancholy moon. She gazed upward into the black sky, seeing the lonely orb in a sea of shimmering stars. The stars captured her imagination and drew her back to the candlelight at the log village.

"Twinkle, twinkle little star." The childhood rhyme played in her head.

Twinkle, twinkle little star.

The melon moon is not so far.

She smiled to herself. The moon was nearer than any other heavenly body. Why did it make her lonely?

God is much nearer, she thought. The words hummed in her head.

"Are you coming? We'll be late." Rose stood at the bottom of the staircase, waiting for the children, as she'd done for the past few weeks since Paul's work had become more demanding.

"Why are you leaving so early?" She turned and saw Paul in the dining-room doorway. "The kids haven't eaten yet."

"I know." She slipped her arm into her coat sleeve. "The church is having its annual pancake breakfast this morning. The offering is used to purchase Christmas gifts for needy families." She shrugged her other arm into a sleeve. "Anyway, the kids love pancakes."

"So do I," Paul said.

She felt her mouth fall open. "I know, but—"

"Can only members attend?"

"No." His question shocked her. "I didn't think to—"

"To invite me." He grinned.

Footsteps could be heard pounding along the upstairs hallway, and in an eye blink the twins bounded down the steps.

"We're having pancakes," Colin said, dragging his tongue over his lips and rubbing his belly.

"Me, too," Kayla said, mimicking Colin's actions.

"Me, too," Paul said, aping them both.

"You are?" Kayla's eyes widened. "Are you really coming, too?"

"You don't mind, do you?" He pointed the question to the children, but Rose sensed he was aiming it at her.

"We'd love to have you join us," Rose said.

Paul held his arms extended at his sides and eyed his slacks and pullover sweater. "Is this okay?"

"You'll be the best-dressed man there," she said.

Rose stepped from the house, amazed that Paul had

joined them. She'd longed to invite him to church, but she'd felt an invitation was out of place.

Since his help had arrived from L.A., he'd fallen back into his old pattern—home late, no time for the kids, no conversation. She missed it. The long hours were reflected in his tired face.

Paul drove, and as she sat in the passenger seat she gazed at the leaden gray sky, but she didn't let the weather darken her spirit. She grinned, thinking if she'd known all it would take to get Paul to church was a meal, she would have invited him to the Mulligan Stew and Bar-B-Cue they'd held a few weeks earlier.

"I'm pleased you decided to come along. It's good for the kids to see you at worship."

"And good for me." He gave her a tender smile. "I know I've been quiet lately. My mind's filled with details, and I'm so talked out at the plant I'm not in the mood when I get home. But we're making progress."

"I assume the L.A. exec has been helpful."

"Absolutely. Gretchen's top-notch. Wonderful. I respect her immensely."

Gretchen. A woman. Rose hadn't considered he'd been spending late evenings with a female. She stared out the passenger window, trying to control her sudden fear. Paul's long days away, his silence, his withdrawal. She knew the day might come, but she wasn't ready for it.

"She'll be leaving right after Thanksgiving. By then, everything should be in place. Then it's a matter of training."

"That's good," Rose said, managing to sound sincere while facing her worst fear. A woman had walked into Paul's life—a woman he admired and respected.

They entered the church through the side door, and the enticing aroma of buttery pancakes and grilled sausages guided them to the fellowship hall. Rose tried to push Paul's startling news out of her mind. She was in the Lord's house, and today she needed solace. They joined the buffet line, then found empty seats.

To Rose's surprise, Paul recognized two men from the plant at their table. After they were introduced, she waited for a raised eyebrow or a questioning look.

"You're a nanny?" one of the wives asked.

"She baby-sits us," Colin said, "except we're not babies."

"Me, either," Kayla added.

Rose grinned at the children, thrilled at Kayla's outgoing nature. The change had been overwhelming.

"I'm sort of the baby-sitter and glorified housekeeper," Rose said, managing a pleasant look while enveloped with a sense of uneasiness. Today she needed nothing else to play with her emotions. She studied the woman's face, but saw nothing but cordiality.

"I never thought housekeeping had any glory in it," the woman said with an amiable grin.

Everyone chuckled, and the chatter continued. Rose wanted to relax, but she couldn't. She forced down the breakfast she, for once, hadn't prepared.

Paul watched Rose with concern. She'd gotten quiet, and he wondered if he'd made a mistake inviting himself to the breakfast, but the reactions of his employees settled over him like a gift. At the office, conversation felt strained, but this morning it seemed spontaneous and congenial. Maybe being in church would create a new bond between them. Believers seemed bound together with special ties. An old hymn lilted into his thoughts—"Blest Be the Ties That Bind." Perhaps those ties were stronger than he had realized.

They ate their breakfast, intermingled with conversation, until the crowd thinned, and Rose motioned toward the doorway. "I'll take the children to their Sunday-school classes. You can meet me upstairs for church."

Paul agreed and followed the worshipers to the sanctuary. Soon Rose arrived, and they found an empty pew. The service began, but Paul's thoughts drifted to his new feelings for Rose. He wished he could put a finger on them. He knew he felt gratitude and—

The truth settled over him. For the first time since Della died, he was looking forward to Christmas. Rose had been the catalyst. They'd become friends. Their lives had become entwined. *Blest be the ties that entwine.* The words twisted in his head.

As they'd spent more time together, Paul had sensed a kind of like-minded spirit they shared. The painting came to mind. They'd both been drawn to it immediately. But it was more than that. He felt comfort in her presence. She exuded compassion and evoked from him a new tenderness.

The congregation rose for the Gospel, and Paul yanked himself upward, aware that he'd been daydreaming.

"Today we will hear a lesson from Paul's letters to the Philippians, chapter two, beginning with verse one." The pastor's rich voice filled the air. "'If you have any encouragement from being united with Christ, if any comfort from His love, if any fellowship with the Spirit, if any tenderness and compassion, then make my joy complete by being like-minded, having the same love, being one in spirit and purpose.'"

Paul's heartbeat accelerated. Hadn't those same words entered his thoughts moments ago—tenderness, comfort, compassion, like-mindedness? He'd been thinking of Rose, but these words applied to Jesus and to faith.

Marriage was about being united, but being united in Christ was beyond his imagination. *Make my joy complete.* Was that what made Christians optimistic in the depths of despair? They found blessings in failure and joy in sorrow? His mind whirred with questions.

He slid a glance at Rose with her chin tilted upward, her eyes straight ahead, her lips curved at the corners. She was beautiful inside and out, and he was blessed to have her touch his children's lives—blessed having her touch *his* life.

Make my joy complete. Rose's face brightened his thoughts.

Snow illuminated by the porch light drifted past the dining-room window. Rose slid the chairs beneath the table and replaced the centerpiece. Everything seemed in order. She'd worked hard to keep Paul's lady friend out of her mind. He hadn't brought her home. He hadn't mentioned anything about her. Rose needed to leave well enough alone until the day came when she'd have to move on.

Tonight the children had settled on the living-room carpet, playing a game while Paul read the newspaper. The house seemed cozy and comfortable, but not her. She had to drive to her apartment alone.

She drew in a lengthy breath and snapped off the dining-room light. Turning toward the kitchen, she was drawn again to the snowflakes settling on the shrubbery outside the window. She stepped back and gazed at the wintry scene. In the darkness, the minute patterns glided downward like confetti from heaven. White and perfect. Beautiful.

"Are you leaving?"

Paul stood so close behind her, she jumped at his voice. "I didn't mean to scare you," he said.

He didn't step back, and she stood where she had been, feeling the heat from his body and his breath rustling her hair.

"I was thinking how beautiful it looks."

He rested his palms on her shoulders. "I like looking at the snowfall, but I'm guessing a full week of driving in it will be about all I'll want."

She felt the warm pressure of his hands and struggled for something lighthearted to say. "Everyone dreams of a white Christmas." Another song rippled through her mind. "Did you ever roast chestnuts on an open fire?"

Paul chuckled and gave her shoulders a squeeze. "No, but there's always a first time." He lowered his hands. "If this keeps up, we'll have a white Thanksgiving."

The holiday caught her attention, and she spun toward him. He caught her shoulders again and stood so close her pulse quickened. She stepped back before she could draw in enough breath to speak. When she moved, Paul dropped his hands to his sides.

"Are you planning to have Thanksgiving dinner here?" she asked.

"I thought so."

"Will you want to invite guests? Your aunt Inez?"

"I hadn't given it any thought, but why don't you call her? Invite friends from church, if you'd like."

His offer surprised her. "This is your family's Thanksgiving, not mine."

Paul shook his head. "You're part of this family. Don't forget that." His gaze captured hers as if he'd read her mind.

"Thank you," she murmured, lowering her eyes.

She could hear him breathing, and she waited for him to walk away. When she found the courage to lift her head, she saw that he was studying her face as if searching for something.

Rose watched his hands rise, this time capturing her arms as they hung at her sides. The warmth of his touch rolled down her limbs.

He looked desperate. "If you would just tell me…"

She felt his hands tense against her arms as he drew her closer. Stunned, she searched his face, his eyes heavy lidded, his chest rising and falling in deep breaths. He lowered his head and his lips parted. Paul's mouth neared hers, and her chest ached with the waiting.

"Daddy, Colin won't let me play."

Kayla's voice invaded the room like an alarm signal. Paul jerked backward, and Rose gulped for air.

Kayla bounded toward them with Colin on her heels.

Rose shifted away. In the kitchen she pulled her coat from the back closet and located her handbag. Before she could call good-night, Paul stood in the kitchen doorway.

"I'll see you tomorrow," she said, avoiding his eyes. "I'll give Aunt Inez a call in the morning. I'm sure she'll be pleased." She stepped toward the back door.

"It's probably slippery out there. Are you sure you want to drive into town tonight with this—"

"I'll be fine," she said.

"If you're sure."

As she put her hand on the knob he said her name, and she turned toward him.

"I suppose we should invite Gretchen for Thanksgiving dinner. She's away from home."

"Sure thing," she said, giving the door a push. The wind caught it, and Rose struggled to keep the door from tearing from its hinges. She stepped from the porch into the wet snow. It sifted into her shoes and covered her ankles.

"Be with me, Lord," she whispered, not sure if she were talking about the drive home or about what had happened inside the house.

Chapter Eight

Paul hadn't felt normal since the night he'd nearly kissed Rose. He couldn't stop replaying the moment and asking himself over and over what he'd been thinking. The answer was always the same. Rose and her smiling eyes.

He hadn't been able to loosen her image from his thoughts, not since the night at Historic Log Village when he'd seen her face illuminated in the candlelight. Even before that. Days seemed to meld together like a collage of wonderful moments. Rose had brightened their lives.

But now he had to decide what to do about it.

Struggling with his dilemma, Paul let his gaze drift to the sleeve of photos he'd taken in the backyard weeks earlier. They'd been lying on the table, and he hadn't looked at them since Rose had brought them home.

He opened the packet. Emotion washed over him. He gazed at the twins mugging for the camera, their faces shining in the autumn sunlight, their clothes sprinkled with leaves. He shifted the top photo and, beneath, sat his own picture with his beautiful children beside him.

Next he saw Rose cuddling the twins while love filled

her eyes. He paused, afraid to look, afraid to see what was coming. He inched the top photo away and looked. Rose again. Each one touched his heart—her smile, her happiness, her face glowing with contentment. He slid a photo into his shirt pocket and placed the rest back into the sleeve.

Paul stood and moved to the window. Outside, the leaves were gone. Beneath the leaden sky the earth looked cold and hard, but his life had been warmed by a woman who'd been his children's nanny for nearly two years. What would he do now with these growing feelings?

He'd been blind.

The scent of turkey filled the air as Rose removed the potatoes from the burner. She'd been in a daze for the past three weeks, trying to make sense out of Paul. She'd truly thought that he was about to kiss her that night. The ride to her apartment had been a nightmare, between the unfamiliar slippery streets and the events that had brought on a tangle of fantasy, reality and disbelief.

She and Paul hadn't spoken of it since that evening. So often, Rose wondered what might have happened if Kayla hadn't barged into the room. She'd been prepared for his kiss. She longed for it, yet she knew it wasn't meant to be. It could only have added to the confusion already in her heart, especially since she'd learned Paul's friend was a woman. Now she was coming for Thanksgiving dinner.

When the doorbell rang, Rose let Paul answer it. Voices drifted in from the foyer, and Rose's heart lodged in her throat. Prayer had helped her with the struggle. Only God promised to be faithful forever, and Rose couldn't blame Paul. He'd asked her to be his friend—nothing more than that. And she'd realized this woman might also be only a friend—maybe a beautiful, shapely friend, but those were things Rose couldn't control.

"Rose."

She straightened as Paul's voice sailed through the dining room. She could see their shadows moving across the white table linen before she saw them.

"Rose," Paul said again, coming through the doorway. "I want you to meet Gretchen Thomas."

Rose managed a smile.

"Gretchen, this is Rose Danby, my right arm…and my left one, too."

When she saw the woman behind Paul, Rose clamped her jaw to avoid showing her surprise. Rose had expected a young, shapely woman. Instead standing in front of her was a tall, large-boned woman whose hand was extended toward her.

"It's nice to meet you," Rose said, accepting the woman's handshake.

"I've heard so many wonderful things about you," Gretchen said.

Shame washed over Rose as she gazed at the woman's once-blond hair, now streaked with gray. She'd never thought Gretchen would be a woman executive in her fifties, but Rose could only guess that's what she was. "I'm glad you could come. Eating alone on Thanksgiving isn't easy."

"I've had to do it since my husband died," she said. "We were married nearly forty years."

Nearly forty years. Rose did her math. Unless the woman had married very young, she had to be in her sixties. "It must be difficult."

"We can get used to anything as long as we have our faith," Gretchen said.

"Can I help you do anything?" Paul asked.

Rose shook her head. "We'll be eating shortly. I'm just about ready. You go ahead."

Paul took Gretchen's arm and steered her back through the dining room. Their voices faded to a distant hum.

Ashamed of herself, Rose leaned her back against the kitchen counter and covered her face. "Lord, what can I do?" She'd judged a situation that she'd known nothing about.

Living with distrust and jealousy was destructive. She'd become too involved in the family and knew she needed a life of her own, a husband and children. She'd never have these staying in Little Cloud.

If she couldn't get her emotions under control, she had no choice but to leave. Jan had told Rose she was always welcome if she decided to return to L.A., and Rose truly missed her friend. Maybe this was God's way of pointing her back to California.

While Paul was giving Aunt Inez a ride home with a bag of turkey-dinner leftovers, Rose helped the children with their baths, then convinced them it was bedtime. They grumbled until she teased them about the broom, and they giggled as they obeyed.

The scent of turkey filled the house, giving her a homey feeling. The meal had gone well, and she had finally settled her ragged emotions and enjoyed Gretchen's company. She could see why Paul respected and admired the woman.

She settled on the sofa, recalling her fluttering heart as her arm had brushed against Paul's while they worked in the kitchen. They'd been preparing dessert—he making coffee, she whipping cream. Since the night of the near kiss, they'd become like strangers at a bus stop, apologizing for getting too close and avoiding each other's eyes. The change felt frightening, but it made her think.

Tonight she decided to talk with Paul if she could find the courage and the opportunity. The chance would arise when he returned from his aunt's. In a way she felt better having made the decision.

By the time Paul arrived, the house was quiet. Rose had her legs curled beneath her and a blaze in the fireplace.

"Thanks for the fire," Paul said as he came through the doorway. His coat was littered with newly fallen snow. He slipped it off and shook it, then vanished.

Rose heard the entry closet door open and close, then footsteps as Paul came back into the room. "It's snowing again?" Rose asked, uncurling her legs and rising.

He nodded. "Just a few flakes, though."

Paul settled into a chair by the fire while she remained standing. He grew more handsome every day, and the reality broke her heart. Tonight his light brown hair looked disheveled from the wind, and his close-cut shave had begun to shadow. She longed to touch his jaw and feel the prickles of the whiskers that bristled on his cheeks.

"Are you leaving?" he asked.

She motioned toward the window. "If it's snowing, I probably should go." But that wasn't what she'd planned to do. Her commitment to talk to him niggled in her mind.

Instead of leaving, Rose returned to the sofa. "Do you have time to talk?" She sat on the edge of the cushion.

"Talk? Sure."

She lowered her gaze, not knowing where to begin. The words clung in her throat, unwilling to leave until she forced them out. "We don't usually talk about personal things, but I want to tell you something so you understand why I react as I do."

"Is this about the other night?" he asked.

It was the first reference he'd made to the incident, but

she didn't want to start there. She had too much to explain before that ever happened.

She shook her head. "When I first came here, you said you needed a friend. I certainly needed one. I had no way to make friends, since I wasn't working in the community. But sometimes I'm not sure…" She faltered, knowing she had to back up to start the story where the problem had begun.

When she looked up, Paul was giving her a questioning look. "I hope you didn't misunderstand me," he said. "I never meant anything inappropriate when I asked you to be my friend. I—"

"I know that, Paul." Suddenly she felt foolish. Why confess the humiliating experience with Don? "Never mind. Let's forget it."

He leaned forward. "No, please. I want to hear what's bothering you. I thought it was the proposal or something else I'd said or done. The other night when—"

"It's a combination of things," she said. She sent a quick prayer that the Lord would help her tell the story without bitterness or embarrassment. She so often felt guilty for what had happened. Yet she had been faithful, as God commanded. Don hadn't.

She began, controlling the old hurt that clashed with the present. She made it brief, and when she stopped she studied his face. "So you can understand why I have a problem with trust…and judgmental people."

"Yes, and thanks for trusting me. I understand now. I know you have a strong faith and high morals. I'll always respect that."

He stood and crossed the floor, sinking beside her on the sofa. "But I wish you'd told me before. You've been suffering in silence, and I've probably stepped on your toes a million times without knowing what you had gone through."

She shrugged. "It just takes me a while to come to grips with most everything."

"You needed a friend you could trust, and then I walked through the door in L.A. and proposed to you without explaining what I had in mind."

"That did undo me. Don had been my boss, and I've promised myself never to mix romance and work."

Paul flinched. "No wonder you were upset."

"And I've never understood how you could propose to someone you didn't know well or didn't care about."

Paul pressed his hand against her arm. "Don't think that, please. I cared very much about you. You were excellent with the twins. They loved you. I admired your ability and respected you as a person. I thought that perhaps—"

"But you didn't love me."

Paul jolted backward, hearing her words. "No, I didn't, but I…" After what she'd said, how could he ever tell her now that his feelings were different? He'd spent every waking hour thinking of her and the twins, imagining how they were spending the day, envisioning Rose's smile waiting for him when he came home, her gentle voice when she met him at the door.

"You say you respected me, but I don't see it."

"What do you mean?" His pulse tripped.

"If you respected me, you would have known I would never marry a man who didn't love me fully. Not for convenience, not for money, not for comfort or security. I'd rather be single."

"I wish you wouldn't say—"

"I'd rather be childless." She turned to him. "And I want children more than anything else in the world."

Childless? Seeing the look on her face, Paul felt his heart break. He couldn't imagine Rose single and childless for the rest of her life. One day a man would sweep her off her feet, and lately he'd wished he could be the one to do just that.

Chapter Nine

Rose leaned against the kitchen counter and wondered what she was doing. Prolonging the agony was her answer. She'd fallen in love with the children, and worse, she'd fallen in love with Paul.

He cared about her. She accepted that. He'd been kind and generous. He'd included her in family activities and told her she was important to them, but as she'd said the other night, she was his employee. That would never change.

And she would never be available for another man as long as Paul was in her life. So what about marriage and children? The answer hung on a thread.

Christmas was only three weeks away, and she needed to prepare the family if she were really going back to California. The quicker the better, as far as she was concerned. As soon as the thought entered her mind, a knot formed in her chest. *Heavenly Father, please let me hear Your voice.*

She heard nothing but the twins banging something from the front of the house.

Her thoughts drifted back to Gretchen. Rose had been

mortified when her jealousy had caused her to concoct a romance between Paul and the woman. Every time the memory resurfaced—and it did often—she cringed.

Jealousy, distrust and frustration had become her way
of life, and they were not the attributes of a Christian.
She'd asked God to guide her, to give her courage to leave,
then her heart would tell her to stay.

Since Gretchen had returned to L.A., Rose was pleased
that Paul had done what he'd promised. He'd been arriving home on time again. She knew it would be good for
the children after she was gone.

Gone? Is that what she would ultimately do?

Her only defense had been keeping busy, planning for
Christmas and wrapping the children's gifts. She'd hidden
them everywhere she prayed the twins wouldn't look.
Today she'd put her energy into baking cookies. She'd
have a supply that would last through January.

Rose wandered into the living room and put on a CD of
Christmas music. The holiday carols filled the room and
wrapped around her heart. She checked on the children,
who'd decided to conspire in Paul's study about what they
wanted to give their father for Christmas. They'd been particularly well behaved in the past week, and Rose assumed
their goodness had to do with Christmas.

Though she'd written to Jan that she was giving serious
thought to going back and had even received a lively telephone call filling her in on all the news and giving her encouragement, Rose couldn't envision actually walking out
the door. The thought made her ill.

Yet the idea persisted. Though she would miss the twins,
the possibility of getting married and having her own children softened the hurt.

Before she left Little Cloud, Rose wished she could be

honest with Paul about her feelings. But what good would it do? She'd only embarrass herself and face his rejection. A woman should never fall in love with her boss. The relationship was doomed.

The buzzer on the oven sounded, and Rose's heart lurched. She opened the door and pulled out two sheets of plump sugar cookies. She'd bought decorator frosting, and once she covered the cookies with a white glaze, she planned to let the children help make the designs.

As the new aroma sailed into the air, she heard the sound of two pairs of feet thudding nearer. She watched the doorway, and in a heartbeat the twins appeared.

"More cookies?" Kayla asked.

"I thought you liked cookies," Rose said.

Kayla leaned over the pans and sniffed. "We do, but you've made lots already."

"I'm stocking up." Rose's throat tightened.

Colin eyed the icing tubes. "Can we help put on the decorations?"

"Once they cool." Rose shifted the cookies to cooling racks, then set the sheets in the sink. "Did you decide what gift you want to buy for your dad?"

Kayla nodded.

"What is it?"

Colin plopped his hand over Kayla's mouth. "A surprise, but we need little round macaronis."

His request threw Rose. What would they do with macaroni? "I'll pick some up for you the next time I'm at the grocery store."

"Okay," Kayla said. "Buy a big box. We're going to make something."

"Make something. That's wonderful. Your daddy will love that more than—"

A noise caught her attention, and all eyes shifted to the outside door.

Paul stepped into the kitchen in his stocking feet. "Mud," he said.

Colin pointed. "Rose will get the broom after you."

Paul wiggled his toes. "No shoes. I'm safe."

Rose grinned at their antics.

Paul sniffed the air, then ambled to the table and snatched a cookie. He took a big bite and licked away the crumbs. When he turned, he gawked at the filled containers piled on the counter. "We're having a bake sale?"

"We're stocking up," Kayla said. "And don't eat any more of those, Daddy. We're going to decorate them."

"I'm sorry," he said, meandering across to the counter that held the plastic bins of cookies. "Are you decorating these?"

Rose shook her head and watched him slip out another. "You won't be hungry for dinner."

"Yes, I will. Paul Bunyan can eat a million flapjacks." He grinned. "Or something like that."

Rose eyed him. "Paul Bunyan?"

"Paul Bunyan's a lumberjack," Colin said, peering at Rose.

"I know, but what's that have to do with anything?"

"We're cutting down our Christmas tree tonight," Paul said.

"We are?" The twins whooped and bounced across the floor to Paul's side.

He gave them a hug, then looked at Rose. "Don't worry about dinner. We can pick something up while we're out."

She nodded, having lost her spirit for cookie baking. The Christmas tree. The emotion seemed too much for her.

"You'll come, too," he said, as if he sensed what she'd been thinking.

"No. I think I'll—" She stopped herself. She wanted to decline, but sitting home alone was the last thing she wanted to do tonight.

"You're coming along," Paul said. It wasn't a question.

Rose nodded. "Do we have time to ice these cookies?"

"By all means. I have to change clothes, and then I can help, too."

When he was gone, Rose pointed the children to their task. She put on the glaze, and they decorated. By the time Paul returned, they were giggling at their mistakes and praising their successes.

Paul pitched in, and soon the cookies were finished and spread out over the table to dry.

Within minutes, they bundled up and headed out the door. Paul drove to the restaurant first, and when they'd finished eating, they were on their way. Rose still hadn't gotten used to the miles and miles of forest that lined the roadways. In L.A. a tree off a freeway was a rarity. As she watched evergreens blur past her window, she figured they could have stopped anywhere and laid an ax to a pine or fir.

About thirty miles from town Paul pointed to the sign— Willard's Tree Farm. The temperature had dropped in the past hour, and the mud had frozen. At the tree farm the car bumped along the compact ice and snow as if it were on an old corduroy road. The few flakes that had twirled past the windshield earlier had grown to a full snowfall. Rose hoped they'd dressed warmly enough.

After they parked, Paul pulled a handsaw from the trunk and headed toward the cashier's shed. The kids frolicked beside him while Rose trudged behind, her heart vacillating between sorrow and joy. This Christmas had become so special to her—not because of her leaving, but because of the closeness she felt to all of them.

The attendant pointed out their options, and soon they were trudging across the frozen earth toward the trees. "Douglas fir? Balsam? Scotch pine? What's your pleasure?" Paul aimed his gaze at Rose.

What was her pleasure? She drew in the pine scent that filled the air. This moment was her greatest, surrounded by the people she loved and entertained by the snowflakes flitting from the sky. They caught in Paul's hair and lashes. The children twirled in circles, their tongues sticking out to catch the infinitesimal crystals.

Though the night was cold, Rose warmed at the sight of it all. "I like real Christmas trees with big gaping holes and short needles. The kind I had when I was a kid."

"You mean the ugly kind?" Paul's voice was filled with teasing.

"Beautiful ones," she said, swinging her fist to poke his arm.

With the momentum of her punch, she lost her footing on the slippery ground. She felt her legs sail out from under her, and all she could do was protect her arms and head from being injured. She smacked against the ground on her backside.

Kayla darted forward, concern wrinkling her smooth face. "Help her, Daddy," she cried.

"I'm fine," Rose called out to halt their worry.

"You don't look fine to me," Paul said, coming to her rescue. He reached down, clasped both her hands in his, braced her feet against his heavy shoes and pulled her upward.

She stumbled against him, her breath making a cloud of white mist that mingled with his in the cold air.

When their eyes met, Paul let her go.

"No, Daddy," Colin said in his directive voice. "You have to hold Rose up so she doesn't fall again."

Paul shrugged as if the boss had spoken. He clasped Rose's waist and held her close to his side.

Rose felt enveloped in protection and love. The children romped in front of them, pointing to trees and chattering like squirrels. Finally Rose spotted the tree between the feathering snowdrops. A beautiful tree, almost perfect, with widespread limbs and open places to hang large ornaments.

She slowed and pointed. "That's it. That's a real Christmas tree."

Paul let his arm slide from her waist and moved closer. He read the tag. "It's a Fraser fir. They say it doesn't lose its needles."

"That's what we want," Rose said, thinking of the housecleaning.

The children agreed, so Paul stepped forward, bent low and drew the saw back and forth. Rose watched the tree until Paul called, "Timber." As it tilted, Rose scooted in and caught the fir before it hit the ground.

While she carried the saw, Paul hoisted the heavy tree over his shoulder, and they made their way back to the hut. He had become Paul Bunyan as she watched him walk along, his back so straight he seemed taller than usual, his strong arms balancing the tree on his shoulder. The vision made her ache.

The attendant bagged the fir, and as Paul paid the cashier, she ushered the children to the car. The snowfall grew heavier. In moments Paul joined them, and while he mounted the tree to the car roof, she buckled Kayla and Colin into the back seat. Before she could open the passenger door, Paul stepped beside her and laid his hand on hers.

"I'm glad you came. It wouldn't have been fun without you," he said.

She sensed his sincerity and something deeper in his

eyes. The look sent her reeling. "That's because I fell and made you all laugh."

He tilted her chin upward, and she felt snowflakes settle on her nose and eyelashes.

"No," he said, "it's because you're as much a part of this family as I am." His hand slid up to cup her face and he leaned closer and kissed her cheek.

Rose's skin tingled, and his words swirled through her mind as wildly as the snowflakes. *Heavenly Father, why can't I hear You?*

She heard nothing but Paul's breathing.

Chapter Ten

Paul sat in his study, looking out the front windows.

He'd kissed Rose's cheek two days earlier, and he couldn't lose the memory. He relived the moment his lips had touched her face. He'd felt the cold of the snowflakes, but the warmth of her skin had melted his heart.

During the past days he'd faced where his emotions were leading him. He would sometimes pause in the kitchen doorway to watch her. How he longed to sneak up behind Rose, wrap his arms around her waist and kiss her graceful neck…but his dreams stopped there. Until he felt assured Rose would accept his advance, he'd keep his place, as she kept hers.

With possibilities tossing in his head, Paul wandered to the front window and leaned on the casing. He'd always disliked winter, but again today snow drifted down like feathers from a torn pillow. The view from the study inspired him. From the turret he could look out four windows into the wooded landscape across from the house. The bay window would make a perfect location for their tree.

Tonight Rose had mentioned hanging the Christmas decorations. He grinned, thinking about the electric candle boxes he'd seen stacked on the living-room chair, and he could picture one in each of the study and dining-room windows that looked onto the front. He was curious what else she'd bought that he didn't know about.

Hearing the telephone jingle, Paul headed toward his desk, but the ringing stopped. Rose rarely received a call, so he left the study to see if it was for him. He heard her voice from the kitchen telephone, and he paused in the doorway.

"Thanks for inviting me."

Inviting her? His chest tightened, and he waited.

"No. Really. I can't. It's impossible."

Instead of eavesdropping further, he walked into the kitchen and leaned against the door frame. Rose's face was flushed, and he knew something had upset her. A deep urge washed over him, and he longed to hold her in his arms.

"You're very kind. Yes. Thank you." She hung up the telephone, and when she turned around, she gave a start.

"Sorry," Paul said. "I thought the call was for me."

She shook her head, a frown furrowing her face.

"Is something wrong?"

"No, not really."

He knew differently, but he hoped she would tell him. Paul's concern grew. He crossed the kitchen and touched her arm. "You're annoyed about something."

Her eyes darkened when she looked at him. "I should be complimented, I suppose. A gentleman from church asked me to go with him to dinner and the Historic Home Tour."

His pulse quickened.

She turned away. "I said no, naturally."

Was that natural? She didn't date. She longed for children and marriage one day, but she'd said no. As her employer—her friend—Paul knew he should encourage her to go out with the man, but he couldn't respond to her in either capacity. He could respond only where his heart led him. "You said no because of the children?"

"It's not the children, Paul."

He searched her eyes, wanting to probe. "I was just curious."

"I know," she said, her voice as disillusioned as the last kid picked on a baseball team.

He stood there not knowing what to say and knowing he should say nothing. He shoved his hands into his pockets and wandered across the room to the refrigerator. He stood in front of it, not hungry but yearning for something.

"Why did he call *here?*" Paul asked before he could stop himself.

"I work here. He didn't know my home phone number. It's not listed."

It had been a stupid question. He couldn't look in her eyes, fearing what she might see. Instead, he stared at the floor and dealt with emotions he hadn't felt in years. Frustration, anxiety, jealousy. What would he have done if Rose had said yes to the man?

His mind worked like a calculator, trying to figure which man had called her for a date. He supposed the guy had every right, but it seemed…

His stomach twisted. He had no hold on Rose. She could date anyone she desired. She could do anything she wanted. The possibilities left him empty. Rose had become his life. She was the reason he hurried home. She was all he could think about. The realization etched itself on his heart.

He'd felt it coming like a gentle breeze—no sound, no drama, only an awareness, an airy dance of emotion that touched him almost imperceptibly. He was falling in love with Rose.

"I'm going up to check on the kids and make sure they're sleeping," she said.

Before her words registered, she had vanished. He stared at nothing while questions filled his mind.

How could he have missed what was happening? He knew he admired her. He'd been grateful and tried to make her happy. But was that love? Could he want a mother for the children so badly that he only thought it was something deeper? A voice said no. Could he be responding to the social pressure of having a wife? No again.

His feelings were as real as the tension growing in the cords of his neck. He moved to the stove and turned on a burner, then filled the kettle and set it on the stove.

He heard Rose's footsteps and paused.

"They're asleep."

Alien sensations sizzled through his limbs, and he didn't know what to do or how to react. He gestured toward the kettle. "I'm making tea."

"That sounds good." She sat on the edge of a kitchen chair and ran her hand across the back of her neck as she stretched her shoulders.

"Headache?" Paul asked.

"A little one. I'll be fine."

Paul watched her a moment until longing spurred him to slip behind her. He used his thumb to massage her upper back, then kneaded her shoulder muscles, working his way up to the cords of her slender neck.

Rose gave a soft moan of pleasure as she relaxed against his hands. She tilted her head back and forth, her silky hair brushing against his fingers.

He struggled to keep himself from running his hands

through her locks. The kettle whistled, and he was forced to move away. "Feel better?"

"Thank you. That felt nice."

He focused on making cups of tea while calming his emotions. He longed to tell Rose how he felt. Perhaps he could tonight if he found the courage.

"Let's get comfortable," he said, leading the way. They settled in the living room. Both seemed thoughtful and quiet as they sipped their drinks.

Paul noticed the boxes of candles and remembered their plan. "Are we decorating tonight, or don't you feel up to it?"

Her gaze shifted to the boxes. She shrugged. "It's getting late."

"I'll help you," Paul said—anything to keep her there.

She set her cup on the saucer. "I told the kids they could help me decorate, but I assume they're mainly interested in the tree." She rose and moved to the boxes.

He joined her. "Ready?" His senses were sparked by Rose's nearness. Her fragrance seemed to surround him—the scent of spices and vanilla like the cookies she had baked.

She lifted a box and tore off the wrapper. They worked together freeing the candles, then headed into the dining room and set them in the windows. While he ran after extension cords, Rose finagled a way to fasten them to the windowsills.

When they moved to the study, Paul pulled a Christmas CD from the stack, and the soft music floated through the speakers. When the last candle was attached and lit, they adorned the open banister with green and red ribbons, then attached the wreath to the front door.

"I'll clean up," she said, heading into the dining room. He returned to the study and gathered the empty boxes. Soon Rose came through the doorway with a trash bag, and he dropped the cardboard into it. She knotted the end and he smiled at how organized she was…and how important she was to him.

A prayer entered Paul's thoughts, and he sent it heavenward, asking God's assistance. Rose's sensitivity had become his primary concern. He had to tell her how he felt at the right time and in the right way. He could only pray that she would believe him and forget he was her boss.

Mel Torme's velvet voice filled the room. "Chestnuts Roasting on an Open Fire."

"Remember?" he said.

She searched his eyes and nodded.

"Sounds like a plan," he said, trying to ease the mood. "Dance?"

Her frown returned, and he expected her to push him away, but he persisted. He grasped her hand and drew her into his arms.

The room was lit only by a desk lamp and the soft glow of the window candles. His pulse accelerated.

Rose felt stiff in his arms, but he drew her closer, breathing in her sweet fragrance and feeling the softness of her skin against his. Finally she relaxed and rested her head against his shoulder.

They moved slowly, swaying to the Christmas music, and Paul felt whole for the first time in years.

As the last strains of the song faded, Rose stepped back. Her hand trembled in his, and his gaze was drawn to the look of sorrow on her face.

"What's wrong, Rose?"

She lowered her head, but he'd already seen tears rolling down her cheeks. His stomach tightened as fear slammed against his happiness.

"I've made a difficult decision this evening," she said.

He didn't like the sound of her voice.

"What kind of decision?"

"I'm going back to L.A. It's the only way I'll ever be happy."

Chapter Eleven

Rose's words knocked the breath out of Paul. He gaped at her, making no sense out of what she'd said. "Please don't say that."

"I'm not making idle talk, Paul. I've struggled with this for too long. I believe it's for the best. We can both get on with our lives."

Get on with our lives? What lives? She'd become his life. He opened his mouth to tell her how his feelings had changed and grown, how she filled his life with joy. She'd given him a sense of wholeness, but he searched her serious face and stopped himself from opening his heart.

Rose wouldn't believe him. She would think he'd confessed his feelings so he could keep her there, and she'd promised never to fall for her boss.

The room hummed with silence.

Her misty eyes caught his. She stood so close he longed to take her into his arms again and hold her against his chest to soothe the ache that burned within.

He forced himself to speak. "What will we do? What will the kids do without you?" He captured her arms, his heart ready to speak despite his fears. "What will I do without you?"

She lowered her head and shook it. "Please don't ask me those questions. I'm trying to figure out what I'll do with my own life."

Her life. His heart burned for her, and his prayer rose to heaven begging God for an answer. Did she love him? Could she love him? Questions pressed against his chest like a boulder. He needed time.

"The holidays are here, Rose. Christmas is less than three weeks away. Maybe this is selfish to ask, but could you stay through the holidays?" His hands trembled so wildly he shoved them into his pockets. "Stay for the children. They'll be devastated without you."

He'd be devastated.

His gaze followed the tears that rolled down her cheeks and he reined in the desire to kiss them away. He felt helpless and hopeless. Only God could heal the situation.

Rose inched her chin upward, her eyes wet with tears. "You're right. I shouldn't have said anything now. I should have waited until the holidays were over." She brushed the tears from her eyes with the back of her hand. "I'll stay for the twins."

He rested his palm against her back, almost afraid to touch her for fear he wouldn't be able to stop. "Thank you. This means so much to me."

She looked directly into his eyes. "I'm doing it for myself, too. Your kids mean the world to me."

"You deserve children of your own. I know."

She nodded. "I hope you understand."

"I do…with all my heart."

"We'll have to make the best of it," she said, rallying. "I feel better now that I've told you. We'll get through Christ-

mas, and then I'll try to explain to the kids why I'm going.
It'll give you a chance to find someone to replace me."

Replace her? His body trembled with the thought. "I can
never replace you. Don't even think it. You have no idea
how much you mean to us."

She stepped back. "Don't make it more difficult. Please.
This wasn't a flash decision. I've struggled with it for a
long time."

"What will you do?"

She shrugged. "I don't know. My friend Jan invited me
to stay with her until I get things together."

She'd already spoken to a friend. Pain ripped through
him. She'd really planned this long before telling him. He'd
allowed himself to fall in love, and now…

"I'll keep busy," she said. "I want to do some more
shopping. I have a few gifts for the kids hidden in the
guest-room closet. I've wrapped some during the day when
they're at school."

Her words tumbled together, and he made no sense out
of them. Shopping? Gifts? How could she talk about those
things? His sorrow veered toward anger. "You shouldn't do
so much for them."

"Why not?"

He had no answer, except that she was leaving them. In
a heartbeat Paul realized he was angry at himself, not Rose.
She'd given her all to them. He'd given her so little. *Lord,
help me to show my love. I'm lost already.*

"Paul Stewart, please." Rose waited, her ear pressed to
the telephone and concern pounding in her head. Then she
heard his voice.

"Paul, this is Rose." She swallowed.

"Is something wrong?"

"I'm worried about Kayla. She hasn't gotten up from her nap this afternoon. She's running a temperature, and she's very listless."

"What's the problem?"

"I don't know for sure. Colin seems all right. I called the pediatrician, and he wants me to take her to Emergency if I can't get her fever lowered."

"Emergency?" He paused. "I'll come home now. You'll need help with Colin."

"Thank you," she said. "Be careful. It's snowing heavily over here."

"I'll be careful."

Rose clutched the telephone to her chest long after Paul hung up. She feared she was acting overly concerned. Children got sick—that was part of life. But this time her worry had reached its peak.

Only hours earlier the children had hidden themselves away with the macaroni. They'd needed their safety scissors and glue, and Rose couldn't imagine what they were making.

When she'd noticed Kayla's discomfort, Rose had given the child aspirin. Now she'd given her more with the doctor's orders, and all she could do was wait. If that didn't work, she would bathe Kayla in cool water. Her next concern was not alarming Colin. He'd already hovered nearby while she telephoned the doctor, and he looked worried.

The snow had begun to fall early, and in the past hour it had increased. The wind had picked up, and the flakes were flying at a wild angle, leaving snow piled against anything standing.

Christmas filled Rose's mind. It was only three days away, and its coming meant she would be leaving soon. Though she'd professed leaving would be the only way she could be happy, her heart fought against her decision.

Each time she looked at the children, she was stunned by the emotion that rattled her. She loved them like her own, and the longer she stayed the more she cherished them. She'd thought leaving would bring her happiness, but now she sensed nothing could.

"What can I do?" Colin asked from the doorway.

"You can give me a hug," Rose said.

He plodded across the room, his arms dangling like a chimpanzee, and wrapped them around her neck. She drew in the scent of his laundered T-shirt and the peanut butter and jelly he'd eaten for lunch. Rose knew he was concerned about Kayla, and so was she.

"I have time to play one game," Rose said.

He grinned and ran from the room. Rose trailed after him, in no mood for games today, but she needed to keep Colin distracted as well as herself.

They played a game of concentration, and Rose was so distracted that Colin won legitimately. He jumped around the room, cheering as if he'd won an all-star game. She pushed herself up from the floor and tousled his hair. "Let's go up and see if Kayla's awake yet."

"Is she sick?" His questioning brown eyes, the same color as Paul's, searched hers.

"A little," Rose said, hoping she sounded convincing, "but she might feel better now."

"Did she take her aspirin?" he asked, striding beside her up the staircase.

Rose nodded.

When they entered Kayla's room, Rose's hopes died. Beads of perspiration covered Kayla's nose and forehead.

"Could you do me a favor?" she asked Colin, hoping to keep him busy.

"What?" His gaze was directed at his twin.

"Would you help me run water in the tub? We have to make it cool. Not icy cold, but cool."

He looked puzzled.

"Do you understand? We need to use the water to help get Kayla's temperature back to normal."

"Not cold. Cool," he repeated.

She nodded, then grabbed the thermometer and put it under Kayla's arm. She counted, then checked Kayla's temperature. One hundred and four.

Rose beckoned to Colin to follow her, and they headed for the bathroom. Rose turned on the tap. "Now you check it for me, okay?" she said to Colin, his face so filled with concern it broke her heart. "Remember, not cold, but cool."

Colin placed his hand in the water. "It's good," he said, looking at her as if to make sure he'd done the job well.

Rose felt the water. "Perfect. You're doing a good job." She touched the side of the tub. "When it reaches here, I'll turn it off."

"Is Kayla okay?"

"She'll be fine." *Please, Lord, we need Your help here,* she prayed as she waited for the tub to fill before turning off the tap.

When she returned to the bedroom, Rose slipped her arm beneath the child's neck and called her name. "You need to wake up, sweetheart."

Kayla gave a soft moan, her eyelids fluttering.

"I know you feel terrible, but I want to get you into the tub so you can feel better." She eased Kayla up, her body limp, her arms flopping at her sides. Though Rose was slender, fear made her strong. She maneuvered Kayla into her arms, then straightened her back and headed for the doorway.

Outside she could see the heavy snowfall continuing. She pictured Paul trying to drive the two-lane highway to the house, and she feared for his safety, as well.

When she entered the bathroom, she sent Colin to watch TV, then undressed Kayla and slid her into the tub. The child reared upward when the cool water washed over her, but Rose held her firmly and began to sponge her while sitting on the edge of the tub.

After a while her back ached, and she wondered if she had the strength to lift Kayla out of the water. She reached for the bath towel, and in her peripheral vision she saw motion.

"How's she doing?"

Rose's heart leaped when she heard Paul's voice. "I don't know. I'm praying she's better."

He moved to her side and rested his hand on Rose's shoulder. "If you move, I'll lift her."

She breathed a sigh. "Thanks. Somehow I got her in there, but I wondered how I'd get her out."

While Paul lifted his daughter, Rose wrapped her in a towel, and Paul kissed Kayla's cheek, then headed toward her room.

Rose stood a moment, enjoying the sense of relief that rushed through her. Paul's presence made her strong again. She might be an employee, but she loved them all as if God had meant them to be a family.

The stress of the day caught in her throat and pushed behind her eyes. She drew in a deep breath to calm her thoughts.

Paul glanced over his shoulder, looking for Rose. She looked tired and strained, and he couldn't thank her enough for what she did for the twins. He'd been surprised to see

Colin enrapt in a television program. Before he came up the stairs, Colin had reported that he and Rose had played a game, and he'd helped her run the water. She was so good with the children. Like a real mother.

If only... He let the thought fade. Only God could solve what seemed so impossible.

In Kayla's room Paul set her on the bed, wondering if he should leave her in the towel or find clean pajamas.

"Let me," Rose said behind him. In moments she'd taken the wet towel from Kayla and dressed her in a nightgown, then pulled up the sheet.

Paul stood beside her holding the damp towel and looking down at his sleeping daughter. "How's her temperature?"

"It was a hundred and four, but I want to take it again." She tucked the thermometer under Kayla's arm and checked her watch. Then she focused on him. "How was the driving?"

"Horrible. If I hadn't started home when I did, I wouldn't have gotten here. They're announcing travel advisory warnings on the radio, and the snow isn't going to stop for a while. They're calling it a blizzard."

"I saw it through the window," she said. Her gaze fell to her watch. She leaned down and pulled out the thermometer. "One hundred and one." She released a sigh. "Much better."

She cleaned and stowed the thermometer, then turned to him with relief written on her face. "Thank You, Lord."

He nodded. "I can't imagine us trying to get her to Emergency in this mess."

"Let's just hope the fever stays down." She brushed her hair from her forehead. "I suppose I should think about dinner."

He touched her arm and smoothed her hair with the other hand. "Let me worry about that."

A faint smile curved her mouth. "No pizza tonight."

His heart swelled seeing her smile, as meager as it was. "You don't think I can cook? Have you forgotten the meal I made for you?"

"Hmm." She eyed her watch, then gave him a generous grin. "I think that was three months ago. Do you still remember how?"

Paul slid his arm around her back and guided her out the doorway, then gave her a wry look. "But what's in the house to cook? I only have a small repertoire."

She spurted a laugh, the first he'd heard in days.

"Okay, Chef Stewart. I'll play assistant and show you a thing or two in the kitchen."

Paul felt the Lord smiling down, and he sent up a rousing thanksgiving. If nothing more, the horrible day had drawn them closer. If God were willing to move mountains, maybe Rose would realize their ties were not only bound, they were tangled around their hearts.

Chapter Twelve

"You can't go home, Rose. Van or not, you'll be sitting in some ditch with no one to help you."

Rose let her arms drop to her sides. "What do you want me to do?"

He shook his head, amazed at her morality. "I think God would understand if you stayed here tonight. We have the room, and you know—" he prayed that she did "—I would never do anything—"

Rose stopped him. "I know. It's my upbringing. I can't help how I feel."

"Your feelings are good ones, but not very practical tonight." He wanted to hug her for her strength of character.

Her expression turned serious. "It's for the best, I suppose. I should stay close to Kayla…just in case."

Paul stood to stretch his overfull belly. They'd cooked a delicious meal of pasta and vegetables, but everyone's focus was on Kayla's absence from the table.

"While we're stuck here—" he gave her a gentle smile "—why don't we set the tree in the stand? It'll give it a day to spread out so we can decorate it."

"It'll pass the time," she said, but her face showed her concern. "I hope Kayla's able to help tomorrow." She shook her head. "I tried to get her to eat, and she's still not interested."

"Later maybe." He drew up his shoulders, hoping to cover his own worries. "I'll get the tree, and you get the stand."

Rose stood and headed toward the door. "Where is it?"

"Good question." He glanced over his shoulder. "Get creative."

She laughed again, and the sound was music to him. Colin followed Paul onto the back patio and he let the boy think he was helping. He'd seen worry in his son's eyes, and it broke Paul's heart.

Colin held the door while Paul tugged the tree into the house. By the time he got it to the living room, he was grateful they'd bought the Fraser fir. He looked behind him and saw no trail of needles, just a trail of snow.

Rose hadn't returned yet, but before he left to help her find the tree stand, she appeared, carrying that and a large box.

"What's the box?" he asked, trying to read the red letters on the side.

"Another tree. I hope you don't mind." She handed him the stand and set the box on the floor.

"Another tree?"

"One of those fiber-optic trees that turns all the colors. I thought it would look pretty in the study in the bay window. It'll look beautiful from the front yard."

Paul felt his mouth sag, knowing how his and Rose's thoughts marched side by side. He recalled thinking about the bay window.

After much struggling, Paul settled the tree in the stand, and to his relief Rose declared it straight after his fourth try. He slid from under the branches and strode back to join her. "Straight as a plumb line."

"And now," she said, pointing to the box, "the pièce de résistance."

"You're a pièce de résistance," he said, sending her a wink.

Her smile warmed him. He opened the box and pulled out the fiber-optic tree. Instructions fell to the ground, and Rose rescued them. She scanned the paper. "Do you want to hear this in French, Japanese, or English?"

"If you want this put together right, try English."

He led the way to the study with the tree while Rose read the directions behind him. It was easy to assemble, and once it was plugged in, Paul understood why Rose had bought it.

"Wait until dark. We can sit in here and watch the lights change colors."

We can sit in here. The words charged over him like ice water. In three more days she'd be getting ready to leave. The sorrow felt too deep, too cruel to bear.

Rose couldn't sleep, couldn't stop thinking about her leaving. She'd come here first with trepidation, but in only days, she'd realized how much she'd missed them. And they had missed her. She'd grown to love the strange little town more than she would have imagined. While her love had deepened for the children, her world revolved around their well-being and their lives.

Then came Paul. He'd filled her foolish dreams, and even though common sense told her to stand back and protect herself, she hadn't listened. Perhaps she'd listened, but her heart couldn't follow what wisdom deemed right. She'd dreamed that impossible dream.

When she thought about all that had happened, the

lovely thoughts dimmed with the knowledge she was leaving. She'd agreed to be Paul's friend, and like a friend, he'd kissed her cheek and danced with her that evening in the study as they listened to the velvety Christmas tune—the night she had told him she was leaving.

That night she'd wanted to forget her decision to leave. What if she never had a husband or children—would she be any less happy than she felt right now, tearing herself away from the only place she'd ever felt complete?

Her thoughts made no sense, and she rose in the dark and walked to the window. The wind bent the trees while heavy snow pelted the house, and though she could see nothing but moonlit drifts, she could trace the familiar outlines. The lilac bush, the wooden bench swing where she'd sat watching the children play in the fall. Bushes and shrubs that had become like old friends.

Though Paul had his faults, she'd grown to admire his strength and fortitude. He'd lost a wife, yet he'd fought to meet his children's needs even when his work had been long and stressful.

And he'd shown Rose love, too. Maybe not the kind she wanted, but—

As the wind shuddered against the window, a loud crack followed by a heavy thud slammed above her head. She spun around, frightened. Fearing for the children, Rose wrapped a blanket around herself and darted into the hallway. As she dashed to their rooms, she heard Paul bounding up the stairs.

"What was that?" she asked, trying to muffle her voice.

"I think a tree limb fell on the roof. Is everyone all right?"

"I'm checking," she said, veering toward Kayla's room. Paul turned left toward Colin's.

Rose studied the ceiling in the darkness. She saw nothing and felt no wind seeping through a broken roof. Kayla slept soundly. Rose touched her cheek, thanking God as her hand touched the child's cooler skin.

She turned back and met Paul in the hallway.

"All's well there," he said, "but I'd better check the attic." He opened a door in the hallway and snapped on the light. A dim bulb lit the stairway.

Rose stood at the bottom and held her breath.

Paul appeared again and descended the stairs. "No inside damage, but if that wind keeps blowing, I'm afraid that limb will slide and tear the shingles off the roof."

"You'll have to call the owner," Rose said.

He shook his head. "I decided to buy the house, Rose. I signed the paperwork the other day. I was going to surprise you at Christmas."

Surprise her at Christmas? She'd been the one to surprise him first with her leaving. His words inched over her, leaving her with questions. Why would buying the house be a surprise for her?

She started to ask, then stopped herself. The whole thing was too sad to talk about in the middle of the night. Too sad to talk about anytime, for that matter.

To Rose's delight, the next morning Kayla appeared in the kitchen doorway.

"It snowed," she said, panning everyone with a glazed look.

"How are you feeling?" Paul asked.

"I was sick."

"I know. Are you feeling better?"

She nodded. "But I'm hungry."

Rose stepped from the counter, knelt beside the twin and

wrapped her arms around her. Kayla rested her cheek on Rose's shoulder. "I'm so happy to see you awake, and I bet you are hungry. I was just beginning to make breakfast." She led the child to a chair and patted it. "You sit, and I'll make you something yummy."

"Pancakes." Kayla licked her lips.

"Everyone loves pancakes," Rose said, winking at Colin.

Paul rose and pressed his hand against Kayla's cheek, then kissed the top of her head. "She feels like my regular girl today."

Kayla gave him a goofy look as if she didn't understand.

Paul didn't explain, either. He wandered into the dining room and looked into the front yard. "I can barely see our cars. The snow has drifted six feet high in places."

"Six feet," Rose said as if disbelieving.

"Looks like it," Paul said, returning to the table. "Right after breakfast I need to get up on that roof and check out the tree. We're not going to get anyone out here for days, and I know it's going to tear up the shingles."

"No way," Rose said, giving him her sternest look. "I'll take the broom after you."

The children giggled, but Paul only shook his head. "Okay. I'll let you climb up there?"

If Rose had her way, no one would be climbing a ladder in this weather. "You'll never dig the ladder out in this mess."

"Want to bet?" He stuck out his hand for a shake. "I'm going to get that tree limb off the roof. It's big."

Rose frowned. "Let's talk about it after breakfast."

As the words left her mouth, she realized she sounded like his wife, giving warnings and orders. She had no business telling Paul what he could do. He didn't respond, and she closed her mouth.

The pancakes were consumed as they came off the

griddle. Rose poured more batter until she finally heard their groans that they'd had enough. She sipped her coffee, enjoying the rich flavor and accepting that she'd hopefully get the last pancake. Two were left.

As she sat with her breakfast and a fresh cup of coffee, Paul sent the children to get dressed, then sat beside her. "I know you don't want me on the roof. I understand. But I have to check it out. I promise if it looks like it won't rip off the shingles or cave in the roof, I'll leave it be."

"We can call someone and just see when they can get here."

He pressed his lips together and eyed her. "It's a waste of time. Look at the road. You can't see it, Rose."

For the first time she headed for the front window, and realized Paul was right. The road was lost in the drifts of snow. "Okay. You're right."

He chucked her cheek and walked away. She heard him in the back hallway putting on his coat and boots, then the garage door opened.

"Lord, keep him safe," Rose said.

She hurried up the stairs and met the children coming down.

"Colin, I want everyone to stay inside for now until your dad checks out the tree, and Kayla, I don't want you outside at all today."

They each gave a whiny moan and stomped the rest of the way down the stairs. She let it go and continued to her room to dress in something warm. If Paul was going on the roof, she was going to be next to the ladder.

By the time she stepped outside, Paul had scraped a pathway to the garage. He'd been correct. The drifts that leaned against the house were taller than she was. Rose had never seen snow like this except in photographs or movies.

Paul appeared, dragging the ladder. "What are you doing out here?" He looked surprised.

"You don't think I'm letting you climb on that roof without someone here to hold the ladder."

He shrugged. "I can't argue that one."

Paul propped the ladder against the house, then extended it to its full height. Rose shuddered, looking at how high he had to climb. He stepped away and vanished inside the garage. In a moment he returned with a chain saw, attached to a large strap. He slung it over his head, and her heart stopped.

"Please," she said. "That's dangerous."

"I'll only use it if it's necessary."

She held the ladder, bracing it against her feet in the slippery snow, while he climbed. She watched as he moved upward, one rung after another, until he reached the rooftop. At her angle, she had a poor perspective as to where the tree limb was in relation to the ladder, and she sent up prayers, figuring she'd barrage the Lord with petitions until He brought Paul down safely again.

When he climbed off the ladder, Rose shifted away and backed up so she could see. Her heart rose to her throat when she saw the size of the limb that had fallen. Paul balanced precariously on one knee, his foot propped against the slippery shingles.

He pulled the cord, and the saw sputtered and died. Next time he gave it a stronger jerk, and she watched him teeter until finally he regained his balance, and the saw roared into action.

Rose looked toward the patio door and saw both children with their noses pressed to the glass watching her look toward the roof. She knew she should go to them and waylay their curiosity, perhaps their fears, but she had too many fears of her own.

As she looked back toward Paul, a large piece of limb rolled along the shingles and dropped to the ground, vanishing in the snowdrift. Another one followed, then another. Her prayers flew to heaven, and each time Paul shifted her heart stood still.

Five or six large logs had fallen to the ground, and she tried calling up to him to beg him to let the rest go, but he was persistent and probably didn't hear her with the roar of the chain saw.

With her attention glued to Paul's progress, she caught a motion above his head. She watched in horror as a large mound of snow slid from higher on the roof and, like an avalanche, surged along the shingles, plunging toward the tree limb.

Rose could do nothing. She let out a scream, but it was too late. The snow came so quickly Paul didn't have time to move.

The mountain of white heaved forward, taking Paul and the chain saw with it.

Panic charged through Rose's body as she raced toward his plummeting form. She stopped, her knees weakening as he hit the logs buried in the snow and his frame was embedded in a snowdrift. When she saw the dark blood staining the crystal snow, she couldn't breathe.

Chapter Thirteen

As Rose's knees hit the ground beside Paul, the patio door opened, and Colin lunged toward her.

"Call 911," Rose shouted, praying the boy didn't see the blood spreading across the snow.

Colin halted in midrun.

"Do you know your address?" Rose called.

He nodded and spun around, bumping into Kayla, who was on his heels.

"Kayla, stay inside," Rose yelled as she turned her attention to Paul.

She shifted the chain saw, then cradled Paul's head against her arm. She used snow to clean the wound and saw a deep cut where the chain saw must have struck. Without thinking, she lowered her head and kissed the spot below the cut, and when she pulled away she saw Paul's eyelids flutter, then open.

"Don't move," she said.

"Did you kiss me?" His words ran together while embarrassment and worry rolled over her.

A faint grin curved his mouth, yet his eyes were glazed with confusion. "What happened?"

Before she could explain, Colin shot through the doorway toward them. "Colin, stay out of the snow, please."

The child stopped, bewilderment mottling his cheeks.

"Did you call?" Rose asked.

He shook his head. "The phone doesn't work."

Her heart sank, and she studied the situation for a moment. "Find my purse, and we'll use my cell phone."

Colin didn't move.

"It's probably in the kitchen or maybe in the bedroom where I slept last night." Rose watched him turn again and head inside.

Through the doorway she could hear an argument ensuing between Kayla and Colin until their voices vanished, but she had no time to question why they were at each other.

"Are you going to tell me what happened?"

Her gaze turned to Paul. "You fell off the roof."

"My head hurts," he said, lifting his hand before she could stop him. When he withdrew it, he saw the blood.

"I'm trying to call 911. You'll need stitches."

His concerned expression vanished. "Rose, an ambulance is not going to get through that snow until it's been plowed."

"Then they can plow it," she said, determined to get him help. Again she used snow to wash the wound so she could take a good look. "It's still bleeding badly. I need to get it to stop."

"We have bandages inside. Let me get up." Paul tried to shift, and as he did, she heard him swallow a moan.

"You might be hurt worse than you think," she said.

"And I also might freeze to death. I prefer having a little pain and getting inside."

She forced him back against the snowdrift and kept her eyes aimed at the door. Finally Colin came through with the cell phone. As he approached them, she could do nothing to block the deep red stain. When he saw it, his eyes widened.

"I'm okay, Colin," Paul said. "You go back inside, and you and Kayla can get out a washcloth and towel so I can wash my face."

"And some bandages," Rose added as she pressed the buttons of her phone. Her heart sank when she realized the battery was dead. Her charger was back at the apartment.

She dropped the telephone into her jacket pocket.

"What's wrong?" Paul asked.

"Dead. Not enough power to call out."

"I forgot mine at work," Paul said.

Rose shifted her body, feeling the cold penetrate her slacks. Her legs felt frozen. "I'll have to help you up."

She eased him into a sitting position, recognizing she wasn't strong enough if he needed more support. "Are you hurting anywhere particularly?"

"How about my pride?"

She shook her head, amazed he still had a sense of humor. "Anything else?"

"My leg. Ankle more specifically, but let me try to stand before you panic." He shifted to stand, but she saw the strain in his face.

"Let me get something. Just stay there." She rose and headed for the patio door while both children hovered there, looking fearful.

"Your dad's okay," she said, patting their heads. "He has a cut on his head and maybe a hurt ankle."

Their eyes welled with tears but neither cried, and Rose was proud of them. "I need two helpers. Kayla, find a blanket somewhere, and Colin, bring in the desk chair. The one with rollers. Then I'll need your help to get your dad inside."

The twins moved like lightning, and before Rose had a moment to think, Kayla returned with a blanket and Colin with the chair. "Okay, you wait here," she said to Kayla. "Colin, come with me."

The child slipped on his boots and coat, then followed her outside. Rose maneuvered the blanket beneath Paul, and then she and Colin pulled it like a sled to the patio doorway. The last few feet were difficult, since Paul had removed most of the snow, but Colin tossed some onto the cement and made their going easier.

Inside, while she held the chair in place, Paul used it to pull himself upward. Once settled, she rolled it into the kitchen and worked on his head wound. She sent the children on errands, hoping to keep them busy as she tackled the worst.

"I'm praying you don't have a concussion," she said, "but I think the butterfly bandages will work for the cut."

"You were right," Paul said. "I had no business up there without the proper equipment. I'm sorry."

She grinned, hearing his apology. "Too late for that now, but thanks. Women do know a few things."

"I never doubted that," he said, giving her a contrite grin.

Once the butterfly stitches were in place, Rose turned on the teakettle. "You need to get warmed up and get out of these wet clothes." She needed to do the same.

The children returned and hovered around them, their eyes focused on the bandages and the bloodstains on Paul's collar and matted in his hair.

"I'm fine. Really," Paul said as he tried to stand.

She noted a grimace that flashed across his face, and she knew he'd choked back a yell. "Really. You're fine. That's interesting."

"Daddy," Kayla said, "listen to Rose."

"Or she'll get the broom after you," Colin added.

The children had been clinging to his side, touching him and peering at his face, but the broom comment made them laugh, and Rose felt relieved.

"You heard them. No more misbehaving," Rose said. "I'll wheel you into your room and lay out your dry clothes. Then maybe Colin can help you dress."

Paul looked at her with surprise. "Okay," he said, touching the stitches absentmindedly.

She noted the matted blood. "Later I'll help you wash your hair."

He didn't fight her this time, and she rolled the desk chair into the hallway, struggling as the wheels sank into the carpet, but the twins pushed, too, and finally they maneuvered him into his room. She praised the Lord the master bedroom was on the first floor and not up the stairs as the rest of the bedrooms were.

She followed Paul's directions and located his clean clothing, then left him in Colin's hands.

The chill had permeated her, too, and she hurried upstairs, dressing in slacks and a top she'd kept handy. With dry socks and warm clothes, Rose returned to the kitchen and made a pot of hot chocolate.

When she checked on Paul, he was dressed except for his socks. Colin was struggling to pull them onto his father's feet.

Rose gave the boy a hug and took over. "Hold your breath and hang on." She worked the sock up his foot, and with only a couple of reflexive kicks and one good moan when she covered his left foot, Rose succeeded. She stood back and looked at him. "Not too bad. I think you'll live."

His ankle concerned her, and she prayed he had nothing else seriously wrong that they hadn't spotted. The Lord was merciful, and she trusted Paul to His care.

"You don't happen to own a cane, do you?" she asked.

He gave her a wry smile. "I thought you'd carry one in your handbag. You seem to have everything else."

"Daddy, you're silly," Kayla said, hanging on to the arm of the desk chair.

Rose ignored his attempt at humor. "Think of something we can use for a cane." She left him to think while her thoughts headed elsewhere. "How about an elastic bandage? I want to wrap your ankle. It's swollen and bruised."

Colin darted off, and Rose paused, wondering where he was going.

"I think you'll find what you need in the linen closet," Paul said.

Rose and Kayla pushed the chair back toward the kitchen, and Colin met them halfway, carrying a baseball bat. "Here, Daddy, you can use this to lean on."

"Good job," Rose said, grinning at the child's ingenuity.

She found the elastic bandage and bound his ankle and packed it with ice. Then, relieved, she settled back with the hot chocolate.

"It looks as if we're at the mercy of the telephone company and the road plow," Paul said. "Otherwise we're stranded."

The kids grinned, and Rose realized they didn't mind the problem now that they knew their dad was okay. They had his captive attention until help came.

"Can we decorate the Christmas tree?" Kayla asked.

"Good idea," Rose said. "We'll start it after lunch. Tomorrow's Christmas Eve. We've waited too long."

When they finished eating, the children raced into the

living room, and Rose followed. Together they dragged out the boxes Paul had set against the wall. "Now wait until your dad gets in here."

She returned to the kitchen to find Paul standing with his weight against the baseball bat.

"It hurts," Rose said, seeing the grimace.

He nodded. "I'm sure it's just a sprain. I'll probably feel better tomorrow."

"Let me help," she said, stepping beside him.

Paul rested his arm around her shoulder and used the cane in the opposite hand. "It's nice leaning on you."

"Glad I can help." She wanted to tell him she loved having his arm around her for any reason, but she stemmed the words.

He didn't move, but stood there, and Rose looked at him to make sure he was okay.

"I'm fine," he said, apparently catching her frown. "I was just thinking."

"About what?"

"How it felt to be Sleeping Beauty."

"Sleeping Beauty." It took her a moment for the reference to settle. She felt her skin warm at his meaning. "I'm sorry. It was a reflex. Instinctive."

"Mothering and loving," he said, looking into her eyes. "I would have done the same."

"You mean if I fell off a roof?" Her heartbeat pitched, and she tried to move him forward, but he remained glued to the spot.

"You know what I mean, Rose."

His words sent her heart on a journey, and she struggled to put two coherent words together, but found none. Instead she eased him forward, taking slow steps until Paul was settled in the living room.

She put on another Christmas CD, then strung the lights. Paul sat back with his ice-packed ankle and directed the activities as they hung the ornaments. Rose kept her gaze veering toward Paul to make sure he was all right. He seemed to be, and she sent up a prayer of thanksgiving.

When the last ornament was hung, Rose walked across the room to snap off the lamps so they could view the tree in the darkness. As she passed the bookshelves, her heart stood still. In the place Della's photograph had been, Rose spotted a new one. A picture of her that autumn afternoon. Her face was tilted toward the sun and a red maple leaf had caught in her hair. Amazed, Rose wondered why she'd never noticed the photograph before. She dusted the shelves often. Most important, why was it there?

She turned toward Paul, but he was listening to the children's excited commentary about the tree. Later she might ask, but for now, she snapped off the light and returned to Paul's side.

Their "oohs" sounded in the carol-filled room, and Kayla ran into her arms and hugged her tightly.

"Why am I so honored?" Rose asked, touched by the child's unexpected expression of love.

"I love you," Kayla said, "and the snow kept us all here together so you can never go away from us."

Never go away. Did the child know? Kayla couldn't, but had she sensed Rose's sadness? Rose held back the tears that surged to her eyes. "I love you, too," she said, wanting so badly to say she would never go away, but she couldn't say that to the child.

For the first time that day Rose felt the impact of her future loss. This family, this house, these moments would be gone forever when she walked out the door. Tears pooled in her eyes. Glad she was hidden by the darkness, she brushed them away and excused herself to make dinner.

Alone in the kitchen, Rose sobbed.

Chapter Fourteen

Later that evening Rose packed away the ornament boxes, then shooed the children off to bed. Her mind was filled with the messages she'd heard that night—Paul's cryptic comment and Kayla's open expressions of love.

While preparing their meal, Rose had felt tears rolling down her cheeks as she thought about her decision. Was it better to stay in Little Cloud and face a single, childless life or return to L.A. and leave her loved ones behind? Both meant heartbreak.

Rose climbed the stairs and checked on the children. They'd gone to bed with little grumbling, each excited about the tree decorating and overwhelmed by Paul's fall from the roof. Before she returned to the first floor, Rose located a bottle of pain reliever. She knew Paul was miserable, and she wanted him to sleep well.

When Rose returned to the living room, the lamplight blinked and then returned. "Do you think we'll lose power?" she asked.

"Very possible. The weight of the snow on those lines, especially if it freezes, can be dangerous."

"If this keeps up, it means no Christmas service or Sunday-school program," Rose said.

"We'll hold our own. It's Jesus' birthday."

His suggestion touched her. "Here's some medicine for pain," she said, setting the bottle beside his water glass. "You should take it now."

He reached over and did as she said, washing the pills down with water, then closed the bottle.

Rose crossed the room and opened the fireplace doors. "We might as well have a fire," she said, piling some kindling onto the grate, then lifting on two large logs. She set a fire starter beneath the fast-burning wood and waited for the kindling to ignite. As the fire spread, she settled into a chair across from Paul.

The music filled the room, and Rose leaned back and let the tiring day wash from her body. Paul's fall from the roof had been overwhelming. Fear had raced through her, followed by panic. The experience of both phones not working, no access to the roads, being snowbound in the woods was alien to her L.A. existence. Yet now as she relived the moments she recalled a sense of challenge and adventure. Neither had been part of her California life—except an occasional trying day on the freeways.

Without warning, Paul grasped the baseball bat and stood.

"Don't hit me," she said, eyeing the makeshift cane and sending him a grin.

He didn't respond, but hobbled to the fireplace and lowered himself to the floor, then patted the carpet.

She didn't move, and he patted it again, except she only heard the sound. The lights had flickered and died.

"Let there be light," Paul said from the floor.

The darkness continued, except for the warm glow from the fireplace.

Rose's first thought was the children. Without electricity, the blower would stop on the furnace. "I'll go up and add a blanket to the kids just in case," she said. "Where's the flashlight?"

"Foyer closet," he said.

She fumbled her way beyond the firelight to the closet. Inside she felt the shelf until her hand touched the light. Soon the beam stretched across the carpet, then the staircase as she made her way up the stairs.

Colin had kicked off his blanket, so Rose tucked it in and covered him with a large quilt. In Kayla's room she stood a moment, seeing the child bathed in the moonlight streaming through the window. Rose covered her with the bedspread and tucked it in, then turned toward the light.

Outside, the moonlight bounced off the snowdrifts, leaving the night in a silver glow. Rose looked into the night sky. Once again the full moon hung above her, round and bright like a beacon. In the past months she'd viewed it as a symbol of her loneliness and singleness, but tonight its shimmering aura led her thoughts in a different direction. As its beams brightened the dark earth, it offered rays of hope to the lost. Rose bowed her head. The Lord knew she was lost, and God's voice told her she needed to find her way home.

Paul had watched Rose's flashlight beam vanish into the darkness and now he waited for her return. His chest tightened, aware of the love Rose had for the twins. She thought of them first in every way. His feelings for her had grown beyond his imagination, and he knew he had to convince her to stay with them in Little Cloud. He loved her too much to let her go.

He waited, and in minutes the flashlight rays bounced along the foyer floor as Rose made her way down the staircase. The light swept into the room, with her only a specter behind it.

She came to his side and draped a quilt over his shoulders. Without his asking again, she sank to the floor close to the blaze. "I think they'll be fine. Heat rises, so it's warmer up there than here. Hopefully the lights will be back on in a few minutes."

"Don't be too hopeful," Paul said. "This is Minnesota, not L.A."

She sat a moment until a faint grin curved her lips.

"What are you thinking?" Paul asked.

"Funny you say that. Earlier I was comparing Little Cloud to L.A."

"No comparison," he said.

"No, but I'm not totally convinced one is better than the other."

"Really?" Her comment caused his pulse to skip. "I thought that you were going back because…" His voice faded, having no ending for her reason.

"'Because' has no answer, Paul. I'm a mixture of incongruity. Go. Stay. I said I'm going, but my heart is fighting me all the way."

Her admission hit him in the solar plexus. "Then why? Why would you leave if you don't have a reason?"

"I have a reason. I—I don't understand it."

Paul felt her shudder. "You're cold." He drew the quilt over her shoulders and drew her closer. "Explain this to me, Rose. Please."

The embers crackled; otherwise there was silence. Paul didn't push. He fought his desire to direct the conversation, to beg her again to change her mind, to remind her of the loss the children would have, to confess he'd grown to love her. Instead, he prayed that God's will be done. Paul couldn't make change happen without the Lord's blessing. He'd learned that these past months while going to church and by reading the Bible he'd bought weeks ago.

He'd seen changes in the children. They came home from Sunday school singing songs about Jesus. They talked about their mother in heaven with a new kind of comfort he had been unable to give them. Perhaps a comfort he had never experienced until now.

Rose had led them to the Lord through her strong faith. She had led them into a new world, a complete world he hadn't felt in years.

She stirred, and Paul felt her draw in a deep breath, then release a deeper sigh. He stood on the edge of anxiety, longing to understand. Then she shifted closer.

"It's difficult to explain this, Paul. You know the things that hurt me in the past—that gave me a dislike of gossip, a fear of being rejected again and a horror of being pitied again. I feared even you pitied me."

He opened his mouth to speak, but he sensed she had more to say and he swallowed the words.

"I realize it wasn't pity. You were motivated so much by the love of your children. Your proposal, your pleading for me to come to Little Cloud and your begging for me to stay."

"Rose, it was that, but now—"

She pressed her hand on his arm. "I was motivated by the love of your children. I adored them, but…" Her voice faded, and her body trembled.

"But…?" He held his breath. What did she have to say that was so difficult? He lowered her head to his shoulder and nuzzled his chin against her hair. He longed to open his heart, but he sensed Rose had to speak first before he told her the truth about his feelings.

"I loved your children from the beginning. Dear Kayla

with all her problems, and Colin with his need to control. They are dear to me, but something else kept me here when wisdom told me to leave."

Paul lifted his head and captured Rose's chin in his palm. He turned her head toward him. "What kept you here?"

"My heart."

He stared at her, bewildered by her meaning. Her eyes searched his and her meaning struck him as pure and perfect as a snowflake.

"I fell in love with you."

Her whisper brushed past his ear, and the words washed over him. "You love me?"

"That's why I have to leave. I didn't believe it at first. I tried to think it was only my imagination. I admired you and respected you—especially how much you adore the twins."

"I've always admired and respected you, but I realized that—"

"Then when I heard that your L.A. executive was a woman, I realized how envious and untrusting I'd become. I thought—"

"Gretchen? Gretchen's like a mother to me."

"I know that now, but when I heard they'd sent a woman, I concocted a romance in my mind. When she was coming for dinner on Thanksgiving, I thought that you were bringing her home to—"

"To introduce her as my lady friend?"

Rose nodded. "I'd misjudged it all, and I knew that I couldn't stay here without ruining my life and yours."

"But Rose, you can't ruin my life now unless you leave. You're what makes life important to me and to the kids."

"You're too kind, Paul. I understand, but I felt I had to tell you." Exposed in the firelight, tears glistened in her eyes.

Paul leaned nearer and kissed away her tears.

"Dearest Rose, I'm not just being kind. I've loved you for so long. One day it all struck me. Our lives aren't complete without you. I was afraid to tell you how I felt because I'd already bungled with my proposal. I knew how you felt about employer-employee romances, and I feared you'd think I was manipulating you to stay."

"Please don't say that now, Paul."

"Don't say it? I have to tell you how much you mean to me. I've asked God to help me find a way to show you."

She lowered her head, then as if struck by a new thought she raised it. "When did you put out the picture of me? The one on the shelf?" Her hand gestured toward the cabinet.

"A while ago. I'd had the photo, but needed a frame."

"I hadn't noticed," she said.

"I hoped you would. You looked so lovely that day. I knew even then that you were special to me. It took me a little longer to realize the woman I'd dreamed about was right under my nose."

"But we're too different. That's part of the problem. You're educated. You've traveled. I'm only—"

"You're only wonderful. You're a born mother. You're a tender woman with love in your heart. You're beautiful, Rose. You're wise and intelligent."

Her eyes searched his as if trying to believe.

"You kissed me today. I had hoped that it meant what I wanted it to, that there is hope for us."

A bewildered look settled on her face, and Paul prayed that God would help her to understand and believe. "Don't pull away from me now. Believe me. Trust me."

"But you're my boss. I work for you."

"Rose, you're fired."

He tilted her mouth upward, her lips full and pliant, and

he lowered his mouth, drinking in her softness and warmth. He'd been alone with no desire for a wife, only the longing for a mother for his children until Rose stepped through the doorway. Then life changed.

He drew Rose closer, deepening the kiss. Rose yielded to his mouth, and she raised her hand to his cheek and brushed the stubble of his whiskers.

At that moment Paul experienced the deepest love that only God could give.

Rose gazed into his eyes. "Let me think, Paul. I'm overwhelmed. I need to grasp all that's been said tonight."

"Trust me, please. I love you."

She nodded, then stood and turned on the flashlight. "I'll help you to your room." she said.

Paul rose and grasped her arm as they followed the beam to his room. After he'd climbed into bed, Rose and the light vanished while Paul lay in darkness.

Chapter Fifteen

The morning light filtered through the window, and Rose sat on the edge of her bed. All night she'd relived Paul's words. He said he loved her. She felt amazed. Part of her wanted to believe and part of her couldn't.

She opened her Bible, asking God's wisdom. She remembered Paul talking about the Scripture that had moved him to realize how much God loved him. She flipped through the pages, scanning Philippians until she spotted the verses Paul had mentioned. "If you have any encouragement from being united with Christ, if any comfort from His love, if any fellowship with the Spirit, if any tenderness and compassion, then make my joy complete by being like-minded, having the same love, being one in spirit and purpose."

When they'd talked, he'd mentioned that human love could be guided by the same qualities—tenderness, comfort, compassion, fellowship and like-mindedness with one spirit and purpose. Wasn't that what she and Paul had done?

In so many ways their relationship was based on the qualities in those verses. Could God have blessed them with this special love? She loved Paul, and she prayed that God would help her accept the truth.

Rose bowed her head, and as her prayer rose to the Lord, she was struck by reality. Whether Paul loved her or not, she knew what she had to do. She rose in the chilly room, dressed and headed to the kitchen, grateful for a gas stove. By the time breakfast was ready, the children and Paul had joined her.

"How's your ankle?" Rose asked, afraid to look in Paul's eyes.

"I have a good nurse," he said. "I'm feeling pretty good. I might go out and see if I can move some of that snow."

"Don't push yourself," she said.

After breakfast they bundled up, and the twins charged out the door to make a snowman. Paul followed, but paused beside Rose, worry filling his face. "How did you sleep?"

"Not well, but I'm fine. I read the Bible this morning, and I've made one decision."

"A decision?"

"I'm not leaving. I'm staying here even if I'm the kids' nanny forever."

Paul grasped her hand and brought it to his lips. "They'll grow up too fast, Rose. Nannies aren't forever. Mothers are."

He turned and stepped through the patio doorway.

Rose's heart tripped. His words were true. *Nannies aren't forever. Mothers are.* She cleaned the kitchen, then made her way to the hidden gifts and wrapped the last of them. Finally she wandered down the stairs with a load of packages to put under the tree.

"Rose, come outside."

"Come and see what we made."

Kayla's and Colin's voices drew her to the patio door. They beckoned, and she grabbed her coat and hurried outside. When she saw their surprise for her, she faltered.

A snowman stood in the yard, adorned with mop-top hair. Rose recognized her flowery silk scarf at its neck and her broom in its hand.

"You made a snow lady," Rose said, grinning at their ingenuity.

"It's a snow mommy," Kayla called.

"A snow mommy." Rose's voice was a whisper. She hid her tears behind her laughter, wiping her eyes with her fingers.

"Look," Colin said. He pointed to a strangely shaped red spot against the snow mommy's chest.

Studying it, she saw it was an apple carved to make a heart.

Kayla giggled. "It's you, Rose. We gave it a heart because hearts stand for love, and you love us."

"I do," Rose said, crouching and opening her arms to the children.

They came barreling toward her, and with their exuberant embrace, she tumbled to the ground as they toppled over her.

"And we love you," Colin said between giggles.

She hugged the children, fighting the tears that rolled from her eyes.

Paul stepped to her side and offered his hand. "Me, too," he said softly in her ear as she stood.

Rose brushed the snow from her slacks, feeling Paul's arm wrap around her shoulders.

"This is serious now," Paul said, brushing his lips against her hair. "We have to talk."

Paul descended the staircase, pleased that the electricity had been restored earlier in the evening. The children had gone to bed filled with excitement that tomorrow was Christmas Day, and he felt his own kind of anxiety.

He crossed the foyer and looked into the living room, where Rose sat on the floor beside the fireplace in the same spot they'd sat the evening before. The room was lit with the fire's glow and the glint of the tree lights.

His stomach tightened as he entered the room. Rose turned to face him and patted the floor beside her. He stood over her looking down at her slender frame and watched the firelight glint in her tawny hair.

Tonight she looked relaxed, not stressed, as she'd been so often in their crazy mixed-up relationship. Employer-employee-friend. What had he asked of her? Yet she'd come through as the dearest friend in the world. The dearest woman in his life.

He sank beside her and took her hand. "You're staying."

"I am."

He brushed his finger across her cheek. "Do you know that I love you?"

"The kids love me. I saw that today." She lifted his hand to her lips and kissed his fingers.

"And what about me?" he asked.

"I love you. I told you last night."

He stood and drew her up into his arms. "I love you, Rose. The kids love you and I do. You've given us more than anyone could expect. Your time. Your concern. Your love. You've made our lives complete."

He held her against his chest, his arms wrapped around her waist, her lips so near he could taste the mulled cider they'd drunk earlier. "You've made me whole, and now it's your turn. I want you to be my wife."

Her eyes searched his. Then her lips curved into a smile and she closed her eyes, then opened them. "This isn't a dream?"

"It's the whole truth. The beautiful truth. Remember

once I promised you anything to come to Little Cloud. To-night I'm promising my love."

Rose took him by the hand and led him to the window, where the Christmas moon spread its silver light over the snow, and pointed. "You promised me that once. Remember?"

"I guess I did promise you the moon."

"But you gave me even more. You gave me the sun and stars. The whole universe."

Rose looked into the heavens, then back at Paul washed in the silver glow. The man in the moon shone down on them, just as Rose knew God had smiled down on them and guided their paths.

Paul reached into his pocket and pulled out a small box. "It's not a ring. We're still snowbound, but it's an early Christmas present for you."

Rose's heart skipped as she took the box. When she opened it, the gift amazed her—the bracelet she had admired weeks earlier. He'd bought it that long ago for her. "It's beautiful."

She dangled it in the moonlight, admiring the fused translucent glass. "Is this an engagement bracelet?"

"If you say yes."

"I do," she said.

Paul wrapped her in his arms, and his lips touched hers. She rejoiced in the wave of happiness that rolled through her. After the long struggle, God had given her the gift to trust and to believe there was one man who truly loved her.

"The kids," she said once their lips had parted. "What will they say?"

Paul didn't answer, but kissed her again.

Torn wrapping paper spread across the living-room floor. Two new bicycles stood beside the tree, while wooden puzzles, new clothes and games sat nearby. While Christmas music drifted from the speakers, Rose held the macaroni-edged picture frame in her hand. The twins had used markers to color the pasta and Paul had bought the frames. She gazed at the photograph of Paul and the children that they must have taken from the sleeve of photos. They'd given Paul one of her with them in the leaf pile. Their homemade gifts touched her heart.

"Rose and I have one more gift for you," Paul said.

The children dropped what they were doing and looked at him with curiosity.

Her pulse tripping, Rose shifted beside Paul, and he wrapped his arm around her waist. "Last night I asked Rose to be your mother and my wife."

Their gazes shifted to Rose's face.

Rose felt tears welling in her eyes. "I said yes."

"Yes," Colin said, jumping up and bounding toward them.

"Our real mommy?" Kayla asked. "Not a snow mommy."

"Snow mommies melt," Rose said, crouching down to hold Kayla in her arms. "I don't melt. I'll be here forever."

Kayla's eyes widened. "Forever."

Forever, Rose thought, holding the child in her arms. Forever, like the promise of the amazing Christmas moon.

* * * * *

Love Inspired

Texas Hearts

Sometimes big love happens in small towns....

A PERFECT LOVE

BY

LENORA WORTH

Things couldn't get any worse for city gal Summer Maxwell—her car broke down just as she was returning to her family's small Texas town to heal her battered faith. A handsome stranger coming to her rescue was a welcome surprise. Yet a secret from Mack Riley's past might end her trust in him…and end their love story, as well....

Don't miss A PERFECT LOVE
On sale December 2005

Available at your favorite retail outlet.

Love Inspired
SUSPENSE
RIVETING INSPIRATIONAL ROMANCE

YULETIDE PERIL

by Irene Brand

Hoping to start a new life for herself and her younger sister,
Janice Reid moves to Stanton, West Virginia, to take possession
of a house her uncle left her. But Janice soon becomes the target
of harassment and threats, which threaten both her newfound
security and her developing relationship with Lance Gordon.

"Irene Brand pens a heartwarming romance with a strong message."
—*Romantic Times BOOKclub*

Steeple
Hill®

**Don't miss *Yuletide Peril*
On sale December 2005**
Available at your favorite retail outlet.